AGAINST THE ROPES

AN UNBRIDLED ADVENTURE

by

CINDY MCDONALD

AGAINST THE ROPES

For information call: 304-285-8205
or Email: cindys.mcdonald@gmail.com

Designed by Acorn Book Services

Publication Managed by Acorn Book Services
www.acornbookservices.com
acornbookservices@gmail.com
304-285-8205

Cover designed by Todd Aune
Spokane, Washington
www.projetoonline.com

SBN-10: 0989180417
ISBN-13: 978-0-9891804-1-2

Printed in the United States of America

For my dear friend, Linda Taylor.
Thank you for telling me how good I am when I am good,
and for telling me when I need to be better. You're insights are
always an inspiration to me.

Acknowledgements

I wish to thank many people who had a hand in the publishing and pre-publishing process of *Against the Ropes*.

My dear friend and confidant, Linda Taylor, who always reads my manuscripts before they go to my editor—thank you for all of those wonderful "suggestions" of yours—I don't know what I'd do without them! I wish to thank my wonderful publishing manager, good friend, and fellow author, Lauren Carr, for her constant support and insightful editing; and the creative genius behind this fabulous cover, Todd Aune. Thank you to those at Acorn Book Services who worked behind-the-scenes on my behalf.

Last but certainly never least; I want to thank my husband, Saint Bill. Your love and support always takes my breath away. Thank you.

Against the Ropes

Table of Contents

I myself am made entirely of flaws, stitched together with good intentions.

~ Augusten Burroughs

AGAINST THE ROPES

AN UNBRIDLED ADVENTURE

~ PROLOGUE ~
ON THE EDGE

Gravel spit from the tires of Punch McMinn's red Dodge Ram pickup truck while it rambled along the desolate dusty road.

In the intense August heat, a dirty haze ascended along the horizon. Begging for a drink, the leaves on the maple trees turned upward to the heavens. The crystal blue sky refused to show any answer to their prayer for storm clouds to rumble through.

Punch had promised Eric West, the patriarch of the West family, that he would rebuild a wall in the old broodmare shed before the autumn chill would be a welcomed relief from the dry hot summer. When you made a promise to owner of the most lucrative Thoroughbred horse farm in the area, you kept it. Disappointing Eric West was never an option.

So, the farm manager of Westwood Thoroughbred Farm was on his way into Rosemount to pick up blocks for the broodmare shed.

When Punch's father had left his mother with children to feed without any warning, Eric West took the boy under his wing. He gave him jobs at the farm to earn a paycheck, and he saw to it that Punch continued playing high school football with his elder son, Mike.

Punch grew up at Westwood with the West kids: Mike, Kate, and Shane. Side-by-side, they cleaned stalls, lugged heavy water buckets, and groomed the Thoroughbreds to a laser sheen before the horses entered the paddock for a race. A game of hide-n-seek or football always filled their spare time—what little of that they could scrounge. Sunday afternoon or Monday night football with the Steelers on the TV in the West's study was a favorite back then. It still remained a weekly ritual to this day.

The Wests were Punch's second family. His loyalty to Eric and the clan ran as deep as Reardon's Run. They always had each other's back—because that's what families are made of.

In an effort to beat the heat, Punch went to Miller Block and Brick early. The brickyard was located smack-dab in the middle of downtown Rosemount. The chain-link fence surrounding the huge yard appeared out of place in the area that was home to business office complexes, as were the columns and rows of cement blocks and bricks that bordered the perimeter. Miller Block and Brick had set up business in the small dusty town in 1917, before it had become a bustling city with tall buildings and a four lane running through the center. Like the Miller family that owned it, the brickyard was a staple in Rosemount.

Harris Miller was the fourth generation to operate the family-owned business. His daughter, Zoë, was being groomed to take over the reins when he retired. Although he was well into his seventies, Harris hadn't even begun to entertain the thought of sitting in a rocking chair on the front porch. The notion making him queasy, he opened the business every morning by six a.m.

Yep, Punch was trying to beat the heat. But, if the truth was being told, he was also trying to avoid Zoë Miller with his early morning errand. Damn, it was looking like he was going to be unsuccessful at both tasks.

While waiting for several cars to drive by in the next lane before he turned left into the brickyard parking lot, Punch could see Zoë through the window. Oh yeah, she was making an impressive show of shuffling paperwork at the sales desk, but he knew better. Punch sighed. He simply knew better.

Suspicion ripped through him. He was pretty dang sure that one of his *loyal* family members had called to alert her of his impending arrival.

That's another thing family does—meddle.

Punch couldn't decide which West would be that spry so early in the morning:

Shane? Hmmm, it certainly fit his MO, but Punch seriously doubted it. Shane had trouble rolling out of bed in the morning. *I won't bust his balls…yet.*

Maybe Kate was the culprit. He loved the slender, blonde-haired, blue-eyed woman of Westwood. She knew what was best for her West men—including Punch. Last week, she sat him down on a bale of straw to have a little "talk" with him about the virtues of one Miss Zoë Miller. Kate could be most convincing and when necessary, quite conniving, except he had his doubts about the shrewd little matchmaker. For the past several months, she'd been very preoccupied with Dr. Holden Reese. *Naw … not Kate, not this time, anyway.*

But Mike … Oh yeah, he was a morning person—always bright and alert and ready to roll. He was good at playing the innocent one—steering clear of other people's business. Yeah, he was as innocent as a fox in a chicken coop. Punch had no trouble picturing Mike dialing his cell phone with an ornery grin on his lips the minute he had pulled out of the farm's driveway. *Payback's gonna be a bitch, buddy.*

Zoë was an attractive woman with full lips, pretty blue eyes, and dark blonde hair that drifted over her shoulders. Charming and witty, she had a huge sense of humor, and she was fun to be with.

An armful, she was a full-figured gal. If he let her drag him into the relationship that she obviously desired, he was absolutely certain that she would be a handful.

Actually, Punch felt a tug of attraction to Zoë. He had taken her out to dinner several times. They had a really good time. They laughed, flirted, and held hands. Zoë's good-night kiss was warm, supple, and oh so sensuous. The look in her eyes had gone beyond the simple attraction of a casual date. She had the look of a woman who was falling deeper. He could feel himself falling a little too deep, as well. Yeah, he could picture being with her, if he wasn't afraid that he would fall short of what Zoë deserved out of life.

Yeah, he could picture that, too.

Even though Punch was thirty-three, he wasn't ready for that heavy relationship stuff…nosiree.

Truth be told, if he were to consider a serious relationship, Zoë would be his pick, except Punch felt as though she deserved better. He was nothing more than a farm manager. He made a very good living, but Zoë came from a prominent family.

Punch just plain wasn't good enough for her.

When the traffic cleared enough for him to pull the truck through the brickyard gates, he drove toward the opposite end of the lot—away from the window. Maybe, he thought, he could walk around back, get Harris's attention through the rear gate, and avoid Zoë all together. After the blocks were loaded he would instruct Harris to put the order on the West's account.

It seemed like a good plan.

Stealthily, he slid out of the seat from his truck. Hoping Zoë hadn't seen him arrive, Punch jogged toward the rear gate while ducking down low and keeping his eye on the front door. Geez, he felt as if he was on a covert mission. He was starting to feel a bit silly.

When he saw Harris climbing into the forklift beyond the gate Punch picked up his pace. He needed to get the old man's attention before he started the forklift, or he would have to go through the sales office and face Zoë, which would make his plan for not.

In the short driveway between the chain-link fence and the block building, Punch called through the gate, "Mr. Miller!" Out of Zoë's view and ear shot, he considered himself safe.

Concentrating on starting the forklift, Harris never looked up. The old yellow machine ground, chugged, and coughed. Scowling, Harris persistently turned the key over and over again.

"Punch!" Zoë's voice caught him totally by surprise.

Punch jumped. When he turned, he fell against the gate, which fell open to drag him to the ground. Twinkling, coaxing eyes greeted him when he looked up.

"Oh! Are you all right? Why didn't you come through the office?" Zoë offered him her hand.

Regaining his composure after his fall, Punch climbed to his feet by holding on to the gate that he was certain should've been locked. "I didn't see your car in the lot. I figured you weren't here yet," he lied.

"I drove in with dad this morning. I'm glad I did or I would've missed you," Zoë said while running her eyes up and down his muscled physique.

Zoë loved big men—the bigger, the better. Punch was a huge black man with broad shoulders, massive chest, and arms that bulked out of the sleeves of his T-shirt. His sheer size was daunting, but he was nothing more than a tender-hearted softy. That's what Zoë loved the most about him.

"I'm looking forward to Dan Quaide's barn dance Saturday night," she said. "You'll be there, won't you?"

Punch swallowed hard. He melted into a sloppy puddle when he looked into Zoë's eyes. His throat was instantly dry. "Sure, I'll be there."

"You'll save some dances for me, won't you?" she purred. For no reason other than to touch him, she brushed imaginary dirt away from the front of his shirt.

Now his throat wasn't simply dry. It felt like it was closing. He managed, "You know I will."

"Good. I'll hold you to it, McMinn." She looped her arm through his to escort him through the brickyard gate. "I'll put the block order that you came to pick up on the West's account." She closed the gate between them and secured the lock. Peeking at him through her long lashes, she added, "See you Saturday, Punch."

An hour later, Punch managed to escape the brickyard without a lifetime commitment or bruising Zoë's feelings. Hurting anyone's feelings wasn't Punch McMinn's style. It simply wasn't in him—especially with Zoë.

Sweat dribbled down his temples. Removing his Steelers ball cap, he wiped the sweat from his brow with his forearm and plopped the cap back on his head—crooked. The right side of his mouth sucked in with frustration while he tapped the button for the air conditioning unit. Warm air poured from the vents.

Damn! I meant to fix that last spring.

Time had gotten away from Punch. Now the blazing heat of summer was punishing him for his procrastination.

The rapper, B.O.B, was rapping on the radio that he could use a wish right now. Punch was wishing that some cool air would miraculously blow through those freaking vents.

Not happening.

The truck bumped and rattled over the old abandoned railroad tracks. Glancing in the rear-view mirror, Punch checked the pallet of blocks in the bed of his truck. No trains had traveled the tracks in over twenty years. Even so, the tracks remained in the road as an annoying hump for which everyone forgot to slow down. They would only be reminded of the tracks once they found themselves bouncing on their seats with their brains clattering inside their skulls while swearing at their car's suspension system. The tracks disappeared into the tall weeds to reappear on a rusted-out, boarded-up bridge that spanned the wide white water breadth of Reardon's Run.

The bumping and bouncing in the cab of his truck and the slight rock of the heavy pallet piled with cement blocks was no longer Punch's focus. The dysfunctional air conditioning unit and Zoë Miller was all but forgotten when his gaze fell upon an old Honda Civic smashed against a tree. Ashen steam billowed out from under the hood that curled back almost to the cracked windshield. The driver's side door hung open.

His eyes narrowed and brows pinched together, Punch slowed the truck to a stop. Measuring the wreck with caution, he slid from the seat. He scanned the area while approaching the vehicle.

The dirt road wound into the hazy distance. The locust and maple trees spread their branches overhead, and the sun beat down on the brittle singed tall grasses alongside the road. The air was still and tight in the cloying heat. The only sound was that of the car hissing. The steam slithered like a phantom serpent into the air.

Punch peered into the car. The airbag slumped from the steering wheel. The interior was pristine. There were no personal belongings lying on the seats or the floor. He straightened with his hands on his hips. He lifted one hand to push his ball cap above his hairline and rubbed his fingers over his forehead. "Hey!" he called out.

Surely whoever wrecked the car couldn't be very far.

His gaze fell upon the tall bristly weeds across the roadway. They fell away as if someone had broken through them to go in the direction of the old bridge. Punch followed the newly-beaten trail. He could see the bridge in the short distance, and hear the water slapping over the rocks in Reardon's Run.

Emerging from the brush he came to a dead stop as if someone had splashed him in the face with a bucket of ice water. He gulped down a thick slug of saliva. Warily, he inched his way to the broken and rotten boards barricading the entrance to the aban-doned bridge where a man stood on the other side of the rusted railing.

The man's eyes were fixated on the rushing water far below. His huge hands clenched the rickety railing. Sweat dripped down through the mass of golden curly locks on his head to saturate his red face. In shock, he seemed frozen even though he didn't look injured.

Punch assumed he belonged to the wrecked Honda.

The man on the bridge looked fraught with indecision and angst.

Punch climbed over the boards and quietly made his way to-ward the man clinging to the railing on the very edge of the bridge. The old planking gave beneath his footsteps. Punch wrinkled his nose when he asked, "Whatcha gonna do?"

The man's head jerked toward him. His eyes were as big as dinner plates, and the skin across his hands was stretched so that it looked like his knuckles could burst through at any second. Dripping sweat, his brows pinched in irritation. "What's it look like?" he growled.

Pursing his lips, Punch raised his eyebrows at the man. He peered over the railing to appraise the rushing white water and the jagged rocks in the creek bed. Cocking his head, he expelled a long downward whistle. "It's a long way down there."

The man dared a glance at the water before turning his eyes back toward Punch.

"Ya know if you hit those rocks," Punch said, "it's gonna hurt like hell … while you're drowning, dude."

The man's mouth dropped open a bit. His brows formed a dis-paraging "V" between his eyes. "Good thing you're not a counselor, cuz you suck at this."

"At what?"

"At talking someone out of suicide," the man said.

"Ooh, you want me to talk you out of it?" Punch lifted a beefy shoulder. "I dunno—seems like you've got your mind made up. Right?" He leaned against a rusted flaking bracket and folded his arms over his broad chest.

The man took in a deep disgusted breath. He managed another peek at the water thrashing over the rocks. Tightening his grip on the railing, he grumbled. "Why don't you beat it?" He waited a moment. When he saw that Punch didn't move from his spot, he expelled a sigh. "I can't do anything right. I thought if I slammed my car hard enough into that tree—"

"Damned air bags." Punch interjected.

"Yeah...I tried to shoot myself yesterday, but I flinched." He turned his head so Punch could see a burned graze across his temple.

Punch winced.

The man let go of another sigh. "So I figured I'd jump, but like you pointed out—either the rocks kill me or I'll drown."

"Sounds like a plan." Punch slapped him on the shoulder.

The man gasped while grasping the railing more tightly.

Punch took several steps, and then hesitated before turning back toward him. "Is there anybody you'd like me to call? Family? Friends?"

The man shook his head with a sigh. "No...there's nobody."

Extending his hand, Punch stepped toward him. "My name's Punch McMinn. And you are?"

The man looked at Punch as if his nose had just grown ten inches out of his face. He stared at his big hand. Punch shrugged. "I mean, I gotta know. So I can tell the police whose floating in the creek."

Apprehensively, he let go of the railing to offer his hand. "Eugene...Eugene Strom."

Punch half-smiled. "Nice knowing ya, Eugene." With that Punch grabbed the large man's hand and yanked him toward the inside of the railing.

Eugene wasn't having it. He was big and strong. Wrestling against Punch's grip, he pulled him closer to the edge.

The old railing groaned in distress. The bolts that still barely held it in place jerked around in their rusted and stripped encasements. Punch managed to wrap his arms around Eugene's waist to heave him over the railing. The two enormous men crashed onto the floor of the bridge. The boards that Punch landed on gave way. He fell through the rotten and splintering wood.

Eugene's eyes popped. He scurried on his hands and knees to the edge of the hole. Peering down, he found Punch clinging to a beam above the rushing death drop into Reardon's Run.

Punch's Steelers cap floated in the air. It swirled until it splashed into the waves and was swept away in the quick current.

"H-hold on, buddy!" Eugene called down to him. He scrambled to his feet and dashed to the other side of the bridge to grab some rope. With quivering hands, he secured it to a brace and tossed it through the hole down to Punch.

The rope lowered and then dangled tauntingly in front of Punch. He had to let go of the beam in order to grab the rope that was out of his reach. Biting his lip, he swung his body forward and stretched his hand toward the rope.

It slipped through his fingers.

Swinging back, his hand barely made it to the beam and the grip wasn't a good one. His hands were sweating. Hearing the whipping waters below, he tried like Hell not to look down. *Don't think about falling! Focus on the rope!*

Once again he swung his legs. Hoping that he wouldn't knock himself off the beam, he stretched again for the rope. If he missed this time, he may not be so lucky to get back to the beam. His hand clenched the rope. He dangled at the end for a moment to get his bearings before he began his climb.

It was a thick bristly rope. He could feel the burn of the skin in his palms tearing. Hand over hand, he pumped his legs while he ascended toward the hole from which he fell.

The rope severely ripped his hands. By the time he reached the opening, his hands were slimy with the blood oozing from his palms. It slid down his forearms to drip off his elbows.

Eugene peered at him through the broken floor boards. The dust mites and the flaking rust danced in the air between them. Waving his hands at Punch, he called out, "C'mon dude, just a little bit farther," He reached down through the gap. "That's it. Grab my hand now."

Punch took hold of his hand. Grunting and groaning, Eugene pulled with all his might until Punch emerged through the broken planking.

They collapsed onto the floor side-by-side. Heaving for breath, their chests pumped up and down. Their shirts were saturated with sweat.

"Damn, that was close," Eugene said around a gasp.

Punch coughed as he glanced around the bridge in relief. He took note of the rope tied to the bracket. Bemused, he managed to ask between huffs of breath, "Eugene, where'd ya get the rope?"

"Oh, um … I was gonna try hanging next."

Cindy McDonald

PART ONE

AT WITS' END

~ ONE ~

Wow! The view changed dramatically for Eugene Strom. A few short hours ago, he was staring down at rushing water beneath his wobbly legs. His head was spinning. He was gripped by anxiety.

Now, he was gazing out at young horses frolicking and nipping at each other in lush green paddocks from a cozy swing on the porch of a grand Victorian farmhouse. Long white barns with blue tin roofs rested beyond the fences surrounding the paddocks. When he tilted his head and bent down a bit, he could see a stone bungalow with a steep roof through the tangle of trees on the other side of the farm. Old oak trees lined the long winding driveway. Punch called the farm Westwood. Except for his smashed Honda chained to the bumper of Punch's pickup in the driveway, it looked like a farm that you would see in a magazine.

A black Jeep Wrangler rolled up the driveway from the barn area, and a young sandy-haired man jumped out. He paused to regard the wrecked car. While circling around it, he yanked his sweaty T-shirt up over his head to bare his clammy torso. With a shrug of his sun-freckled shoulders, he meandered toward the porch. Tired and flushed, he lugged up the steps. The T-shirt dangled from his fingertips to slap against the steps during his climb.

He hesitated at the edge of the porch when he saw Eugene on the swing. A bit cautious of the brute, he half-smiled before offering a friendly nod. He then pressed through the heavy mahogany front door.

Eugene was accustomed to apprehension from strangers. His size always put them at unease. He didn't get that reaction from Punch.

Eugene's physique had been a great advantage as a fighter. He would wield his mass and an intimidating expression at his opponent. The fight clubs could rarely find an adversary as large as Eugene to step into the back alleys and abandoned warehouses where he fought. He never had a chance to be a professional fighter. The covert underground fight clubs—that's where Eugene's audience was and where he made most of his money.

When he wasn't fighting, Eugene worked as a bouncer at a gentleman's club in Philadelphia. He didn't really like working at the club. When he was called upon to quash a disturbance, the customer would have second thoughts after they got one look at him. The girls were always relieved when he showed up. The unruly customer typically offered them a hefty tip in lieu of getting his head crushed-in. Eugene was most thankful when they decided to think with their head—instead of their dick.

Taking a deep relaxing breath, he realized that his hands weren't shaking as they had been earlier. He lifted one big paw to wipe his sweating forehead. He was hoping that the heat would cool down soon—real soon.

Tapping his glasses against his jutted lips, Eric West draped his leg over the corner of his cherry desk. With a spatter of gray through his dark hair, Eric was a handsome broad-shouldered man of fifty-five. He had an imposing demeanor and when it came to his family—or his extended family, which included Punch, Eric was no-nonsense.

He was listening carefully to the case Punch presented on Eugene Strom's behalf. Filled with reservations, he glanced over at Mike, who was lounging on the sofa with his fingers laced behind his head.

A younger version of his father, Mike had dark-hair and rugged good looks, with a strong square jaw and piercing hazel eyes. His broad shoulders eased down into lean hips. For Mike, family was the most important thing in life. Punch wasn't only his best friend. He was like a brother.

Eric could see by Mike's expression that he was having the same qualms that he had.

Punch was a soft-touch. Sometimes, the big guy was taken advantage of. He was a glutton for those in need or hurting. It was a great quality for someone whose appearance was so intimidating.

"C'mon Eric," Punch said. "Cut the guy a break. He's really down on his luck."

Eric took in a deep breath, tossed his glasses onto the desk, and crossed his arms over his chest. "But what does he know about working on a Thoroughbred farm?"

Punch shrugged. "What's he need to know? He told me that he used to be a bricklayer. He'd be a great help with the broodmare shed."

"Laborers are a rare commodity nowadays, Dad," Mike said. "We could use the extra help."

Eric was hesitant. He was feeling some bad juju about the situation. He didn't like the circumstances in which Punch had met Eugene Strom. Once again, it was part and parcel to Punch's good-hearted nature. "How do you know he's not going to try another suicide stunt—maybe get someone else hurt?"

"Look," Punch said, "I'll keep a close eye on him. I don't think he really wanted to kill himself. I think he's just in some kind of trouble and needs a little help is all."

Eric looked at him over the top of his glasses. "Has Mr. Strom told you that he's in trouble?"

"No, he didn't really want to talk about it," Punch said.

Reprimand filled Eric's expression and his tone. "You'd better make damned sure that this trouble isn't police-related," he said just as the youngest West walked in.

Shane was wiping the sweat from his chiseled chest with his T-shirt. His sandy hair was moist and his face was flushed from the merciless heat. When he noticed Punch sitting on the arm of the sofa, his crystal blue eyes lit up and his lips curled into an ornery grin. That was Shane, ornery as a freckle-faced kid with a slingshot.

"Hey, Punch, Zoë Miller called a while ago." Shane beamed while watching Punch fidget. "She wanted me to remind you about the barn dance at Quaide's stable Saturday night."

Punch's upper lip wrinkled at him.

Enjoying the big man's uneasiness maybe a little too much, Mike, Eric, and Shane exchanged smug glances.

"What's the matter, Punch? Don't you like Zoë?" Mike goaded his friend.

"I don't need some white woman attached to my ass," Punch said.

Shane chuckled. "I don't think that's what she wants to attach herself to."

Punch glared at him, while Shane unsuccessfully tried to smother his amusement.

Desperate for a change in topic, Punch turned to Eric, who was trying to keep a thin line to his lips. "I'll set Eugene up in the old bunkhouse for now." Quickly, he marched out of the study in an attempt to get as much space between him and the Zoë Miller conversation as possible.

When the front door clicked closed, Shane hitched his chin toward the foyer. "I'm guessing that Eugene is the big guy on the front porch."

"He's Punch's newest fixer-upper." Mike shook his head. "He's always been such an old softy. Constantly nursing a sick barn cat or dragging a stray dog home."

Flinging his T-shirt around his sticky neck, Shane sank into the wing-backed chair across from the sofa. "Remember the dog he took home when he was fifteen? Damned thing had rabies—ended up biting him, and then disappearing." Chuckling at the memory, he lifted his feet onto the coffee table and crossed his ankles. "Punch had to take all those shots."

Mike shook his head with a smile on his lips. "Mmmm, how's the old saying go? 'No good deed shall go unpunished.'"

Letting go of a deep breath, Eric eased into the brown leather chair behind the desk. He tossed Shane a dirty look. The youngest West removed his feet from the coffee table. Satisfied, Eric leaned back and parked his glasses on his nose. "Let's hope this one doesn't bite us in the ass."

Punch and Eugene made their way to the bunkhouse that was located on the east-end of the barn. Punch could never quite figure why the Wests called it "the bunkhouse." They didn't have any cowhands that sat around the table playing cards or sadly strumming on a guitar as the sun sank behind the horizon, while coyotes cried in the distance like on the old TV westerns of yesteryear. The bunkhouse, as they called it anyway, had been mainly used for visiting jockeys.

It was sometimes used when Eric's mother-in-law came to visit. It wasn't so much that Eric didn't like his mother-in-law; he just didn't seem to like the sound of her voice, or anything she had to say. So Eric's late wife, Barbara, always made her mother comfortable in the bunkhouse.

The bunkhouse resembled an oversized doll house. It had blue siding that matched the tin roofs of the barns. The windows were trimmed in white, as was the Puritan-style front door. Back in the day, Barbara used to plant bright red geraniums in the window boxes. That was a long time ago, and that was where the charm of the cottage abruptly ended.

"Home sweet home." Punch opened the door to feel along the wall for the light switch. The light flooded the room to illuminate the fact that the cottage hadn't been used in a very, very long time.

"It ain't Trump Towers" would've been a gross understatement. Cobwebs dangled in the corners. Against the far wall was a single bed covered with a generous coat of dust. To the right of the door was a kitchenette furnished with a dusty table, two chairs, a tiny stove, and an apartment-size refrigerator. There was a white porcelain sink, with a red and white checkered drape across the front. To the left of the door was a wood stove in the corner, two overstuffed chairs, and a small antilog TV on a wooden stand.

Punch pointed to a door toward the back. "That's the bathroom. I'll have Kate bring ya some fresh sheets, towels, and a blanket. A little elbow grease and this place will look like...um, a clean bunkhouse. I'll help ya wipe it up." He opened the window next to the wood stove so that the fresh hot air from outside could mix with the stale hot air inside.

Eugene waved his hand. "Don't worry about it, Punch. You've done plenty for me today." He eased down into one of the chairs near the wood stove.

The pungent tang of old charred logs was mixing it up with the musty closed-up smell of the house. It didn't matter. Totally remiss of the dust lying on the fabric, Eugene laid his head back against the chair. He was happy to be sitting on something soft and comfortable and relaxing. "I just want to rest a little while if you don't mind. It's been a tough morning."

Wondering what could be so wrong in Eugene's life to bring him to the edge of the bridge that morning, Punch regarded the man slumped in the chair. He looked whiplashed. Eugene had told him on the drive to Westwood that he had worked as a bricklayer when he was a teen. Punch was hoping that working on the brood-mare shed might bring back better memories for this man who was at his wits' end.

Business was always slow during the week at the Lanzville Inn, except on the weekends when all the rooms were rented out to the local young people for one-night hook-ups. Rarely did the proprietor of the motel, Al Levin, rent the rooms to travelers. Most out-of-towners took one look at the shabby motel and continued down the road to Rosemount for more comfortable, cleaner, upscale accommodations.

Al didn't give a rat's ass. The weekend crowd was profitable enough and they weren't too picky about the room, which wasn't exactly in line with the latest décor. The Lanzville Inn wasn't the cleanest establishment, but it did provide the best cable service. There was no wi-fi available. Hey, you can't expect top-notch everything for forty bucks a night—forty-five on the weekend.

Al had worked the front desk all night because the night shift clerk had quit on Friday. By eleven-thirty, it was looking like he was going to work the desk all day because the day shift clerk hadn't shown up yet. Geez, it was hard to get good help.

He glanced out the window. Consuela was slowly pushing her service cart along the narrow walkway in front of the rooms. After shuffling along the cracked sidewalk, the old woman stopped to tap on the door to room number eight. Placing her ear to the door, she listened, and then reached her bony hand into her pocket for the key. She unlocked the door, and let herself in. Number eight was the only room to be rented the night before. An old truck driver dragged in around midnight in need of a few good hours of shut-eye.

It was to be a short day for Consuela—a long-ass day for Al.

He would be able to catch some sleep in the chair behind the desk. Most certain that no one would wander in wanting a room in the middle of the day, Al eased into the chair, plunked his feet up on the registration desk, and closed his heavy eyes. His body slumped, his head nodded forward until his chin was almost resting on his chest, and his breathing slowed.

He was only a whisper away from sleep when the bell on the door jingled loud and clear.

His eyes popped open and his body lurched forward. Looking across the top of the desk he found a pair of hard eyes peering back at him.

He wasn't the usual customer. The young man's face was rigid and cold. The snake tattoo on his neck slithered from the back to the front. The ugly serpent hissed with long fangs at the young man's Adam's apple. He wore a bright white wife-beater T-shirt that clung to his slight, yet muscled, torso. His ears were gauged to the point that you could've tossed a marble through the hole. This guy looked like trouble—big trouble.

Burke Dolin glanced around the tiny lobby—if you could call it that. It was more like a walk-in closet with a registration desk pressed against a wall. The desk was made of two-by-fours covered with a plywood plank that had been painted the color brown. The still-life pictures on the walls were faded, and the carpet wore a dirty beaten path from the door to the desk. The plastic potted tree in the corner was blanketed in a hefty coat of dust. The cloying smell of stale cigarettes and cheap pine air freshener hung in the air.

Burke thought the desk was unmanned until an old guy with a grey comb-over and dark circles under his eyes jumped up from behind it.

"Can I help you?" Al asked around a yawn. He was hoping that the tough-looking customer wanted nothing more than directions.

"Has Eugene Strom checked in?" Burke's voice was rough as sandpaper.

"Nope." Movement outside the window caught Al's attention.

Two bruisers waited on the sidewalk. Their wide shoulders were covered in tattoos; their baggy jeans were barely held up by a belt below their ass. While watching over the parking lot, they sucked on cigarettes and blew the smoke out their nostrils.

Disliking the looks of this crowd, Al didn't want to rent them a room. They looked the type to trash a room good, and then skip out without paying for the damages.

Unhappy with Al's answer, Burke growled, "You didn't even look in the register."

"Don't have to. We only had one occupant last night. His name was Deets. He drove in with a semi. Is your friend a trucker?"

"Naw." Burke ran his tongue over his front teeth thoughtfully.

"Lanzville's a pretty small town, ya know. Now, there're lots of hotels in Rosemount. That's about ten miles down the road. Maybe your friend decided to stay there." Al was hoping so. He wanted the thug and his thug friends to move along.

"Yeah... Thanks." With one last glance around the shabby lobby, Burke pressed through the smudged glass door to set off the bell overhead.

Al sighed in relief.

Jay and Chuck turned when they heard Burke slam the motel's front door. His lips were pressed together tightly in frustration. He plopped against the black GMC Terrain and crossed his arms over his chest before letting go of a long breath. "Not here." He scanned the parking lot, and then the road in front of the motel. "Course he probably wouldn't use his real name. He ain't that dumb, I guess."

"Hey," Jay said, "he was smart enough to know to get out of town after he fucked-up the fight. he knew the boss would be mad, and he was smart enough to grab the money from the duffle bag. He's been pretty smart about ducking us for the past how many months. And he's probably smart enough not to hang around this shitty town."

Burke shoved Jay against the car. "Next time we bump into ol' Eugene, you make damned sure you don't shoot him like you did the last time! We can't find out where the money is from a dead man, asshole!"

"This was a big waste of time," Chuck said with a whine. "He ain't never checked into no motel before."

Burke turned to Chuck. "Hey, there's always a first time. He's gotta be tired of runnin', and he's gotta be around here somewhere. The tracker said the car was in this area before it quit working. Find him … Find the money."

∞ ∞ ∞ ∞

Mike had been lounging on the sofa in the study long enough. There was work to be done, and he'd better get to it.

Wolfgang Whitmore had sent him a young Thoroughbred to be trained. The horse was a two-year-old with excellent bloodlines.

What else would he expect from Ol' Man Whitmore? The wealthy bachelor lived in a grand mansion that rested in the middle of a sprawling horse farm in Lexington, Kentucky. He bred only the finest racing stock from only the best stallions that Kentucky had to offer. Problem was Wolfgang had grown rather decrepit in his late eighties and was now resigned to a wheelchair.

His farm manager wasn't doing him any favors by neglecting the young horses of much needed training. It really wasn't his farm manager's fault. The poor guy was seventy-two himself.

It was killing Wolfgang to spend the money to have Bazinga— or Sheldon as Mike called the colt—trained by outside sources. Mike felt sorry for the horse, but he felt sorrier for Wolfgang's next of kin. He could just imagine Wolfgang's nieces and nephews frantically digging up the front lawn after his passing in search of Maxwell House coffee cans filled with the old man's fortune. Wolfgang didn't like banks and conducted all his business strictly on a cash basis. For the past three months, a messenger service would arrive promptly on the first day of the month with an envelope of money—payment for Sheldon's board and training expenses.

Sheldon hadn't come to Westwood in very good condition. Afraid of the colt, Wolfgang's farm manager never took him out of his stall. Sheldon was almost two years of age, and had never seen the light of day, had never touched grass, and worst of all, he had never been away from his mother.

Three months ago, the van driver had to keep the colt tranquilized for the trip from Lexington to Lanzville, Pennsylvania.

Sheldon had been a real challenge since his arrival. Mike fought every day to lead him from one place to the other. Even Punch was struggling to make friends with him. Sheldon was a very intelligent equine, but when he was in the paddock with the other two-year-olds, they would bully him mercilessly.

Poor Sheldon was a social outcast.

Wolfgang called on a weekly basis to harass Mike about the colt's slow progress. "Twenty-five dollars a day," the old cheapskate would grumble. "What am I getting for that, Mr. West? It seems to be taking you a ridiculous amount of time to get him broke to the saddle."

Broke to the saddle? We haven't even gotten that far. Good Lord, we're still trying to get him broke to anything at all. Every morning is an exercise in WTF?

Mike pulled and tugged and pushed and shoved at Sheldon to get him across the driveway to the paddock gate, and then through the gate to join his peers. Sheldon didn't want to leave the security of his stall. He liked the four walls that separated him from the other horses, and the world outside.

The funny thing was that Sheldon would only stand in the far right hand corner of the stall. He never stood toward the middle or the back. Sheldon was an extreme creature of habit.

Shaking his head, Mike stepped off the porch of the Victorian farmhouse.

What a crazy old coot.

A semi-truck pulling a huge horse trailer rumbled through the farm's stone entrance to catch Mike's attention.

Ed Moore's Horse Transportation trailer bumped and creaked down the winding driveway. The tapestry of oaks slid their sinewy branches over the top of the truck and trailer.

Mike's eyes narrowed. He picked up his pace to greet Ed in front of the barn.

The red semi crunched to a stop.

Old Ed Moore slid from the driver's seat. A tall willowy man, he walked with a limp. Even though he spoke in soft tones, he could be quite stern when need be.

"Hey there, Mike." He rifled through the paperwork that he took from the dashboard until he found the envelope designated for Westwood Farm.

"What are you doing here?" Mike asked. "We're not expecting any horses."

"Well, I got one on here for ya from Belmont Park." Ed handed the envelope to Mike before unlatching the trailer door.

The horses inside stomped and rocked the trailer. Wide eyes peered through the windows along the side of the long twelve-horse capacity trailer. Every stall was filled. Snorts and whinnies burst from the confines when Ed yanked the door open.

Befuddled, Mike ripped open the envelope to take out the note inside. Quickly, he unfolded the paper to read. His eyes popped. His hand whipped upward in a motion to signal for Ed to halt. "No! No! No!"

Abruptly, Ed stopped.

"Do not remove that horse from the trailer!"

Ed scratched his head. "What are you talking about? I was paid five hundred dollars to bring this gray gelding here from Belmont. I've got eleven other horses on this here trailer to deliver. I gotta get him out of the way."

"Well take him off somewhere else." Mike said in a firm tone.

Wondering what all the fuss was about Punch walked up behind him.

"Are you gonna pay me five-hundred bucks to take him back to New York?"

"I didn't ask you or *her* to bring him here."

Ed's patience was running thin. "I'm taking him off the trailer, Mike. You and whatever her name is can sort it out. Until then, the grey gelding is all yours." With that, he yanked the trailer door open, disappeared inside, and then emerged with the immense grey gelding known as Charlatan on the end of the lead.

Mike's head fell backward. His eyes closed while he let out a long painful moan skyward.

Charlatan stomped his hooves on the trailer's ramp.

Wearing a toothy grin, Punch slapped Mike on the back, while reaching into his back pocket to retrieved a peppermint. The horse's ears perked when he heard the paper crinkling as his thick fingers fumbled to unwrap the candy. Charlatan snorted and shook his head. Punch tossed the peppermint into the air. Charlatan caught it in his teeth, and then sucked on it with the satisfaction of a child in a candy shop.

Ed snickered at the sight of the horse's satisfaction.

Mike smacked Punch in the chest with the back of his hand. "Don't encourage him!" he scolded. "And what are you doing with peppermints, anyway?"

Punch shrugged. "Who doesn't like peppermints? Besides, I thought Sheldon might like them."

Ed handed Mike the lead. Slamming the trailer door closed, he made haste for the truck before Mike could stop him. The truck's engine roared to a start before Ed pulled away from the barn.

Punch stroked the gelding's neck. "Awe Mike, you're giving the poor guy the impression that you don't like him."

"It's not an impression."

Charlatan snorted.

Mike groaned.

~ Two ~

After his morning on the edge of sanity, Eugene was exhausted. In the cozy chair next to the wood stove, the events on the rickety bridge high above the rapids of Reardon's Run melted away to lull him into a deep sleep.

His eyes jerked open. He lurched forward on the chair with no idea how long he'd been sleeping. Realizing that he was in the cottage on the farm that Punch had taken him to, relief washed over him.

Slowly, he sank back against the chair and took in the bunkhouse. It was dusty, a bit cruddy, yet it seemed friendly enough and would do … until it wouldn't.

He wiped the sweat from his forehead and temples and pushed himself from the chair. Still groggy, he made his way to the kitchen sink and turned on the faucet. He let the water run to clear before cupping his hands to fill them with the cool water to splash over his face. Refreshing, the water shocked him to full consciousness.

There was no towel available, so he let the water trickle down his face and drip off his chin onto the mass of hair that peeked through his open shirt.

For a moment, Eugene studied the cottage's hardwood floors. Then, he marched throughout while pounding his feet against the planking to discover that it was solid.

Hesitating, he bit his lip.

He turned his attention to the wood stove. The heavy door squealed when he yanked it open. He coughed as the musty burnt air greeted him. Choking, he turned his head away while thrusting his arm up the chimney pipe. It was clear. Still coughing and his eyes watering, he slammed the door shut.

Rubbing his eyes, he plopped down in the chair. The room was wide open. There were no nooks or crannies to speak of.

The sound of a large engine passing by grabbed his attention. Outside the front window, he could see a semi-truck pulling a horse trailer toward the stone entrance of the farm. It hesitated before rolling onto the gravel road and then rumbled away.

Scraping his hand over his watery eyes and then across his bristly chin, Eugene decided that it was time to investigate his new surroundings.

∽ ∾ ∽ ∾

Eugene made his way along the paddocks while watching the horses nibble on the grass. The horses lifted their heads to watch the stranger. After concluding that the man was no-threat, they returned to their grazing.

Not so much as a whisper of a breeze fluttered the oaks' turned-up leaves. Gaily chirping to one and other, the birds swooped from branch to branch.

From the barn, Eugene had a better view of the bungalow across the way. Its steep roof covered the porch that spanned the front of the stone house. Plump red impatiens dangled from hanging baskets along the length of the porch.

The front door stood open to allow the air to sweep through the screen door. Along with the breeze was the sweeping trust that no one would do the bungalow harm.

It was amazing to Eugene that anyone possessed that kind of trust these days.

He could hear horses rustling in their stalls—a snort here, a whinny there—no sounds of distress or angst—only normal horse sounds.

Finally, Eugene came to the barn door. He stepped inside. Along a short aisle to his right, he found the office. No one was inside, so he made a left and meandered down the long wide corridor lined with horse stalls on both sides. Some of the stall doors stood open, while others were closed with gates across the front. The horses poked their heads from their stalls to measure-up the visitor. Some of the Thoroughbreds ducked away from his oversized hand when he tried to stroke their heads. Others laid their ears back to display a nasty face.

Best to leave these bad boys alone.

A few welcomed a gentle stroke or two.

Music from a radio filtered softly throughout the barn. A feminine voice wafted down the walkway to sing along with Faith Hill. "I can feel you brea-the….ju-u-u-st brr-eathe…"

Eugene followed the voice until he came to a stall where a lovely blonde woman knelt down next to a tall sorrel gelding.

Her long locks were gathered in a loose ponytail. Her gold hoop earrings glinted in the sunshine that sliced through the barred window toward the rear of the stall. Seemingly comforted by her voice, the horse stood quietly tied to the stall wall.

Her hands dug into a bucket and came up with a thick pasty substance. Completely immersed in her task, she smoothed the paste over the horse's right front leg while continuing her private karaoke with Faith.

Eugene could tell by her voice and her expression that she sang the words with the country star with the same heart-felt sincerity.

His shadow falling upon her alerted her of his presence. Abruptly, she turned to him with question in her crystal-blue eyes. A thin involuntary gasp escaped her lips before she could call it back.

Aware of his daunting appearance, he smiled at her. "I'm Eugene Strom. I'm a friend of Punch."

Her smile was as lovely as her eyes. After offering her clean hand, she seemed taken aback when his hand swallowed hers. "I'm Kate West." She glanced around the barn as if she were looking for backup. "Punch said someone was staying in the old bunkhouse. I'll bring some clean sheets and stuff over as soon as I can."

"No hurry," he said. "Nice to meet you Kate. Um, what're you putting on that horse?"

"It's a poultice. It's for pulled or injured muscles. It works kind of like a drawing salve."

Eugene stepped in for a closer look. "It won't burn him, will it?"

With a giggle, Kate assured him, "No, not at all." She continued to wipe the substance down the horse's leg. The horse didn't seem to mind. It looked easy enough.

"Can I try?" Eugene asked.

She flashed that beautiful smile again before she moved aside. "Sure, but it's messy."

Eugene patted the horse, and then knelt down next to her. "That don't bother me." He submerged his hand into the bucket. It came up with a wad of the paste that oozed between his fingers. He was intrigued. "It's kinda watery and thick at the same time." He wiped a stray golden lock from his brow with his forearm.

Kate nodded while watching him smooth the poultice over the horse's front leg. His tenderness reminded her of Punch, who her father often referred to as *"Saint Frances of Lanzville."*

She felt a tug of regret at her initial reaction to him. Punch was a huge man as well, yet she never felt intimidated or apprehensive around him. Just the opposite: she always felt safe and secure.

"Very good, Eugene. Hey, not bad. You seem to have a way with horses. Not everyone does, ya know."

"Well, I used to work for the circus." From his peripheral, he saw her eyes widen with bewilderment about his claim. "Yeah, I worked with the big cats... the white lions."

Blinking back, Kate cocked her head. Her eyebrows pinched together. She repeated his claim—to clarify. "White lions? Really?"

"Yep. Is that enough?" Eugene asked.

"Uh, huh," Kate dryly murmured.

He stood up to admire his handiwork with a wide smile. The horse looked like it was wearing a blobby plaster cast. His eyes narrowed. "I dunno, I missed a spot right—" He stepped forward to wipe the paste on a bare patch while stepping into the bucket. His ankle buckled. He teetered sideways with his arms flailing in an attempt to regain control of his massive body's equilibrium. The gooey paste spit from his hands to cover Kate's cheeks, hair, and the front of her T-shirt.

The horse's eyes widened. Snorting, he jumped to the back of the stall and danced in place against the wall.

"Wh-wh-whoa!" Eugene finally lost his balance to land on top of Kate. He thrust her backward into a fresh pile of green horse dung. When the bucket became dislodged from his foot, it flipped into the air to plop up-side-down on his back. The thick gooey pasty slime oozed off his shoulders. Clumps dripped onto Kate's chest while she squirmed, winced, cringed, and grunted under the man who was feverishly scrambling to get up.

Covered in the poultice, Eugene looked like a melting Abominable Snowman. He stumbled to his feet and offered a wet sticky hand to Kate, who looked sick while he pulled her up. Manure dripped from the back of her jeans. The poultice dripped from everywhere else.

"I-I'm sorry," Eugene said in a tone of pure humiliation.

Punch wandered into the stall. His eyes bulged at Kate's soiled appearance and her heavy breathing.

She pitched a scowl in his direction. She was trying to count to ten. She didn't make it. She shoved a pasty hand against Punch's chest, which left a gloppy white handprint on his black T-shirt. "These were new jeans. I can't believe the white lions didn't eat him." She pushed him against the wall and tottered past.

Punch blinked back at Kate's odd remark before taking in the huge man covered in paste in the middle of the stall and the horrified Thoroughbred snorting at him from the corner.

"Shit," Eugene said. "Maybe you should take me back to the bridge."

Punch reached for his shoulder. He retreated when he realized that there was no clean place to touch him. "Ah c'mon, Eugene, a quick shower will fix ya right up."

"What about Kate?"

Punch peered out of the stall to catch a glimpse of Kate shaking the paste from her arms while spouting an angry chorus of: ewe, yuck, and shit, as she pressed through the barn door. "Um, I'm thinking she's heading for a shower, too." Punch turned back to note his appearance. The paste slowly fell in clumps to the straw at his feet. "C'mon, let's get you cleaned up. I want to show you the project at the broodmare shed."

∾   ∾   ∾   ∾

In the barn office, Mike was feeling desperate. There was no way that Charlatan was staying at Westwood. The last time that ornery sonofabitch was at Westwood, he did nothing but cause Mike a whole lot of aggravation, and a whole lot of extra work. Just what Mike always needed: extra work.

Charlatan was an escape artist—a very cunning Houdini in horse flesh. He would wait until everyone had left the barn for the evening, when all was quiet. After finishing his oats, he would nuzzle and jiggle at his door's latch until it unhooked. He would then proceed to joggle his stall door until it slid open.

As if that weren't enough, he would travel from stall to stall until he had freed as many as ten horses. The new ex-cons would spend the night wrecking the barn: overturning wheelbarrows, tossing rakes and brooms about, and breaking dozens of bales of hay and straw over the aisle way while helping themselves to extra portions.

Mike bought new latches. Charlatan would open them. Mike built a heavier stall door. Charlatan would manipulate it until finally Mike nailed the door closed. Yep, the next morning Charlatan and his buddies were in the aisle—partying it up.

To make matters worse, Charlatan's antics at the racetrack were beyond acceptable, dubbing the big grey as un-race-able.

After securing Charlatan's stall door as best that he could, he quickly made his way to the barn office to call one Coco Beardmore to insist—no, demand—that she send a van immediately for Charlatan. Coco was the most chaotic woman Mike had ever been involved with. She was also one of the most beautiful women he'd ever laid eyes on. Nonetheless, he had decided that he was going to be firm. He wasn't going to let her sweet talk him into keeping Charlatan for so much as one day. That's right; he was going to tell her once and for all that Charlatan absolutely positively could not stay at Westwood.

The phone on the other end began to ring. Mike was focused except for the sight of Kate draped in white paste passing by the office while muttering curse words. *What the hell?* The phone was on its fifth ring when Punch went by guiding Eugene Strom, who was completely covered in white paste. *Seriously?*

Finally the phone picked up, "Hello, this is Colette. I'm in Saint Lucia with Tom-Tom, so I can't talk with you right now—" Tom-Tom broke into the message. "No, Sugar Plum, you can't talk to them for two weeks." Coco added with a giggle, "Oh, that's right, I'll get back to you in two weeks! Ciao!"

That giggle burned up the nape of Mike's neck to continue through the top of his head. "Two weeks!" he yelled at the receiver after hearing the phone on the other end hang up without so much as an option for a message. He slammed the receiver onto its cradle with an angry grunt. "She screwed me!"

A snort caused him to look up. Charlatan sauntered past the office door. Mike glanced up at the clock: three o'clock. Shit! Evidently, Charlatan wasn't waiting until the barn was closed up for night—the Houdini horror show had already begun.

Mike dropped his elbow to the desk and his chin into his hand.

❧   ❧   ❧   ❧

The shower felt good. Scrubbing away the thick pasty gloop that covered most of his body, Eugene washed away the sweat and trouble from his morning climb on that rickety bridge.

While Eugene was in the shower, Punch went to the main house to retrieved fresh sheets, and a window fan. He also brought him some of his own clothes to change into. Eugene was a little surprised that Punch's jeans and shirt were a tad tight on him. They would have to do until his clothes were laundered.

Eugene figured Punch went to get what he needed so that he wouldn't have to face Kate too soon after their first encounter. After he had showered and they installed the window fan, he and Punch drove a small boxed-bed utility vehicle called a Gator across the Thoroughbred farm to the broodmare shed. The building rested on a hill overlooking the farmhouse and barns.

While the Gator bumped along the dusty roadway, Eugene noticed a pair of binoculars on the console between them. His lip kicked into a salacious half-smile. His eyebrow arched. "What's the binoculars for? You watching that pretty girl through her window?" Eugene jabbed an elbow into Punch's rib.

Chuckling, Punch stopped the Gator in front of a long metal gate. He slid out of the vehicle to open it. "Go ahead and try it. If she finds out, she'll kick your ass into next Tuesday, dude."

"I believe she could," Eugene said with a smile.

Punch slid back into his seat, drove through the gate, and then got out to close it. "There's a big red-tailed hawk that's got a nest in a dead locust tree near the shed." He pointed beyond a group of fat mares watching them from the shade of a maple tree. "I've been watching to see how many little hawks come out of that nest." Punch rolled to a stop in front of a brown barn.

The back of the barn was snuggled against an embankment that had been partially dug away. Part of the rear wall was missing. What remained was braced with two-by-fours. The view of Westwood was spectacular from the hill. The whole farm lay before them: the stone entrance, the winding driveway, the Victorian farmhouse, the barns, and the quaint bungalow that Mike lived in across the farm.

Awe-struck, Eugene stared at the scene.

Punch nudged him. "See? There she is." He pointed to the cloudless sapphire sky.

The immense hawk's wingspan was at least four feet. Forming languorous circles, she glided above them.

Punch watched through the binoculars until she finally perched on the nest that rested in the "V" of two branches of the dead locust tree. Eugene was amazed at the pleasure that Punch took in watching the simplicity of nature.

Punch lowered the binoculars from his face. "No telling how long until she starts teaching the little ones to fly—maybe while we're working on the shed." He lifted his chin toward the barn door. "C'mon. Let's get started on the easy stuff."

With only six stalls, a feed room, and a loft filled with hay, the barn was small.

Eugene followed Punch up the ladder to the loft.

"As you can see the wall under the loft is the one we're rebuilding," Punch said. "So we need to get rid of the hay. We'll toss it down and stack it in one of the stalls until the wall is done."

"Easy enough." Eugene said. "Why are these horses kept up here away from the rest? Kinda seems like they're exiled."

"Not at all," Punch said. "Only the athletes in training are stabled at the main barn. The broodmares have their own pasture and private barn where it's quieter. Then, they don't have to deal with all the fuss at the big barn. The girls like it up here."

They had no sooner tossed several bales to the floor, when they heard the rumble of a truck and the slam of a door outside.

The barn door creaked open.

With his cell phone in hand and a wicked smile on his face, Mike stepped in and looked up into the loft.

Punch's face crinkled with suspicion.

"Hey Punch, phone call for you." Mike tossed him a grin that Punch would normally expect from Satan's side-kick: Shane. "It's *you-know-who*."

Now Punch tensed.

"I'm not here," he said in a loud, threat-filled whisper.

Narrowing his eyes, Mike cupped his hand around his ear as if he couldn't hear him.

Punch scowled. "Tell her," he demanded in the loudest whisper he could manage without combusting.

Mike shrugged. "I can't seem to find him, *Zoë*." He listened for a moment. "I'll tell you what, I'll have him *call you back.*" He threw a look in Punch's direction. "Oh, don't worry. He's got your number. Okay, darlin'. See you later." Mike pressed the button on the phone to disconnect the call.

Punch flipped him the bird.

Mike inquired, "Why doesn't she have *your* number?"

"Because then she'd be calling *me*."

Mike's lips formed a devilish grin. "I'm not sure what your problem is. She's a really nice girl, and she's not bad looking either."

"Good," Punch said. "You date her."

"I would but I'm not her type, *big* guy." Mike turned to make his exit.

"Hey! What did you do with Charlie?" Punch asked.

"Charlie who?"

"Charlatan."

Mike pointed a finger at Punch to scold him. "Don't give him any nicknames other than the usuals, because he isn't staying. I put him out in a paddock with Sheldon. He seemed like the safest bet."

"Okay." Punch turned to Eugene, who was wide eyed over the entire display. "Let's get to it. The day is wasting away."

Eugene grabbed a bale of hay.

Mike turned back to try once more to prod Punch into calling Zoë Miller just as Eugene hurled the bale over the edge of the loft. The bale struck Mike in the chest to knock him several feet backwards. "Ahhh!" Mike yelled when he hit the floor.

Exchanging anxious glances, Punch and Eugene scurried to the edge to look down.

Mike crawled out from under the bale. Dazed, he struggled to his feet, and sucked in air to replace that knocked out of him.

"Mike, are you okay?" Punch called from the loft.

Saying nothing, Mike waved a hand at him while staggering out of the door.

~ THREE ~

Expelling a terse sigh, Dr. Holden Reese slid from the driver's side of his white vet truck. He glanced across the seat at his veterinary assistant, Ava West. With a toss of her auburn hair over her shoulder, she gathered up her silver vet box.

"Stay here, Ava. I won't be long." Holden slammed the truck door closed. His expression was impassive when he walked through the doors of Chip Walker's stable.

Ava pursed her plump lips and raised her left eyebrow. She had been Holden's veterinary assistant for four months. She had been accompanying the young horse doctor into the stables to aid him in caring for the Thoroughbreds.

For the past several weeks, the protocol had changed when it came to Chip Walker's racing stable. Holden would exit the truck without his vet box and command her to stay put. As the weeks passed, she was becoming more and more suspicious.

She liked working for Holden much better than working for old Doc Spears. Holden was easier on the eyes, and his demeanor was tolerable. If she had to sum it up she would describe him as "cordial with a bit of frost on top".

Ava hadn't acquired her present employment through the usual channels. She saw an opportunity and she leapt at it. Oh how she enjoyed watching Kate West writhe every time she bumped into her and crotchety Doc Spears at the track while Ava conducted rounds with Kate's boyfriend, Dr. Holden Reese. Hey, Kate had her chance. She could have dumped the coot and took the vet assistant job with her hunky hottie anytime. No doubt Holden would've welcomed her with open arms—except she didn't. So, Ava scored the assistant's position, and so very much more—Holden's apprehension.

Ava ran her slender fingers through her hair. She glanced at the clock on the dashboard, and then at the sign that hung next to the stable door that read: Chip Walker Racing Stables in old world calligraphy. A mane-tossed horse galloped underneath the curly words. The sign dangled from a scrolled wrought iron bracket. It was quite classy.

Chip was a top-rated trainer at Keystone Downs. Ava's ex-husband, Mike West had no use for him. He alleged that Chip's axiom was: *"better racing through chemistry."* Ava had heard the same remarks from Doc Spears and other trainers throughout the racetrack. As a matter of fact, Chip Walker was not one of Doc Spears' clients. The old horse doctor preferred that arrangement.

Most cunning, Chip managed to block the penalty when his horses spit out a bad test result. He was never suspended or fined.

Infuriated by this, Spears' face would turn brilliant red—like he was about to have a stroke. Unfortunately, he never did.

Wondering what was taking Holden so long, Ava nibbled on her pinky nail. She found it especially curious since he didn't have the vet box. They had plenty of other stables to visit before the races started. Again, she couldn't still the suspicion that rolled through her more and more with their daily stop at Chip's stable.

Finally, the door opened and Holden stepped into the afternoon sunshine. His impassive expression had melted away into agitation. Biting his lip, he glanced across the shed row and spotted

Doc Spears leaning against his truck. The old man was watching him.

Chip followed Holden from the barn. His dark hair shimmered in the sun and his olive skin glowed. He sauntered behind Holden toward the truck. His muscular biceps bulged from his blue T-shirt that stretched across his wide chest. His dark eyes brightened when he caught a glimpse of the lovely redhead sitting in the vet truck. A sultry smile crossed his face when he approached her window. "Hi, Ava. How do you like working with Doc Reese?"

With effort, Ava smiled at him. "I like it fine."

"Mmmm," Chip moaned seductively from somewhere deep in his throat while never taking his eyes off her. "You are one lucky bastard, Doc Reese, dating a beautiful blonde and riding around all day with this gorgeous redhead. You've got your own little piece of heaven. Wouldn't you say?"

Holden's expression and tone turned deadpan. "Yeah, that's me, I'm in freaking heaven."

Chip's sultry grin widened while he ran his finger up and down Ava's arm. She tensed under his calloused touch. He turned toward Holden who was climbing into the truck. "You don't need to stop tomorrow, Doc. I've got what I need—for now."

Holden fired up the truck.

Chip winked at Ava. His eyes oozed with sexual arousal. She wasn't sure if he was fantasizing about her or Kate or—God forbid—both. She felt violated by this man's scorching gaze. "See ya later, angel," he murmured before the truck pulled away.

Relief.

"What's that all about?" Ava asked.

Again, Holden's expression was impassive while he stared out the windshield. He steered the truck slowly through the shed rows of Keystone Downs. He spotted Kate hurrying to jump into Doc Spears' truck. Then, he realized that Ava had spoken. "What?"

"The shroud of secrecy at Walker stables—why do I have to sit in the truck? Why can't I come in?" She wanted him to confide in her.

Holden was always tense around her because of the precarious position that she had placed him in with his lover. She got that. However, they spent a lot of time together in his truck while making vet visits. She yearned for him to talk to her on a personal level during those long days.

Leaning against the door while twisting an auburn lock around her index finger, she appraised and gauged him from across the seat. He was sullen, his disposition much darker now.

It was Chip Walker.

Driving along, passing in and out of the sunlight, the shadows fell and rose across the planes on his face and over the stubble on his chin. He did not look at her when he spoke quietly, "You're my assistant, Ava, not my guidance counselor."

❧ ❧ ❧ ❧

"Where've you been, young lady?" Doc Spears had his pocket watch in hand.

Looking flushed, Kate hurried toward him. Dr. Ben Spears was a no-nonsense individual. For the past forty years, the man started his pre-race rounds on the backside of Keystone Downs promptly at four o'clock, and he didn't like to be held up by anything—especially a tardy vet assistant. Kate was never late. Even so, the first time was one time too many in Doc Spears' book.

"I'm sorry, Ben, I had a little accident at the farm," Kate explained while scrambling up into the truck.

"Is everything okay? You're not hurt, are you?" The old horse doctor asked with furrowed brows.

"No, my jeans took the brunt of it." She slammed the door. "My brand new jeans."

"In that case, let's go. You're twenty-five minutes late." He snapped his pocket watch shut and shoved it into his pocket. "In my day that would've earned a good tanning," he groused.

"Jeez, he's going all *Christian Grey* on me," she mumbled under her breath.

"What?"

"I said ... sorry you had to wait on me."

"Don't do it again." He watched Holden's vet truck across the way. The worrisome crease in his forehead deepened. He hitched his chin. "Isn't that your boyfriend's truck pulling away from Walker stables?"

Kate's gaze followed his gesture. She smiled until she caught a glimpse of Ava in Holden's truck. While she was well aware that Ava worked for Holden that didn't mean that she had to like it. He had asked her to work for him, but she wasn't ready to make that move. She had no right to ask him not to hire Ava, except he never asked her about it at all. It simply seemed to happen. Her lips squeezed into a tight thin line when she answered Doc's question. "That would be Holden's truck. Yes."

"He should stay away from Walker, Kate. He's bad news," Doc Spears said.

"There's someone else he should stay away from—real bad news." Kate settled back into the seat to pout.

Doc Spears pulled the truck forward. He didn't like Holden associating with Chip Walker. He didn't like it at all.

✎ ✐ ✎ ✐

It had been a long hot day at the racetrack. The purple haze of night draped the sky over Keystone Downs. Hope for cooler temperatures was dashed when the heat never gave way to the night.

After the races ended, Doc Spears and Kate trudged through the shed rows to watch over sweaty horses for heat stroke, as did Dr. Holden Reese and Ava. Luckily, the need for medical attention was delegated to the usual pulled muscles, bowed tendons, and unexplained bleeding through the lassix.

Holden was sweaty and tired when he met-up with Kate in the parking lot. Leaning against her red convertible Mustang, she was mopping her face with a towel when he spotted her. Her jade tank top hugged her torso. A small line of sweat dampened the shirt beneath her breasts. Her dusty jeans clung to her slim figure.

He wiped his mouth with the back of his hand. Damn! She looked hot and sweaty and tasty. Probably salty to boot. He couldn't wait to get her to his apartment. "Are you still employed?" he asked.

She looked up in surprise.

"Yeah, I saw that you were late this afternoon, Miss West," he said. *"Tsk, tsk, tsk.* How many demerits did he give you?"

She smirked.

He gave her a look of wide-eyed horror. "Oh, no! Maybe he docked you twenty minutes pay. If you would've taken me up on my offer, I could have found other ways for you to work that off, you know."

"You wish, Dr. Reese." She slid into the driver's seat of the Mustang.

"You're right. I do." Holden dropped into the passenger's seat. "So?"

"So, what?"

"Why were you late?"

"Punch's new friend that I told you about on the phone," she said. "I think his name is Eugene—he fell on top of me."

Holden scowled. "Did he hurt you? Did he do it on purpose? He wasn't trying something with you, was he?"

Kate rolled her eyes. "It was an accident. How did you know that I was late?"

"I saw you when I was pulling away from Chip Walker's stable."

"Mmm…"

"What?" Holden asked.

"Doc Spears thinks you should stay away from him," Kate said. "He called him *'bad news.'* I agree. But he's not the only one that you're hanging around with that I consider *bad news.*" There was no response.

Pulling out of the parking lot onto the road, she looked at him.

His mood had shifted from light to dark. He turned his head to stare at the urban scenery passing by outside the passenger window. His expression was brooding and distant.

The silence stretched between them while she drove and her stomach clenched. She had strong feelings for Holden—feelings that she hadn't felt for a man in a very long time. He was her handsome cowboy doctor. He had been the center of her world for the past six months. They had fun together.

The sex was amazing. Cowboy sex. What she loved about him the most was the spontaneity of his desire. He didn't require a bed for lovemaking. In fact, he preferred other venues: the shower, the floor, the car, his office. She smiled at the memory of a Saturday morning. While she was whisking up eggs to scramble for breakfast, he crept up behind her, peeled her robe from her shoulders to allow it to drop to the floor, and had his way with her on the kitchen counter. It was brazen and even a little rough, the way he kissed her with such possessive fervor. It was hot. Cowboy hot.

For the past several weeks, something had been eating at Holden. His usual easy-going disposition seemed to dissipate to be replaced with irritability and distraction.

Kate worried that it had something to do with that green-eyed manipulative monster that worked for him—Ava.

Is she trying to seduce him? Kate rolled her eyes at the thought. *Oh, what a shock. As usual, one man just isn't enough for that rapacious bitch.* She wasn't sure if that was bothering him. It was definitely bothering her.

She rolled the Mustang to a stop at the light at the intersection in front of Rosewood Commons, which was where Holden lived. She glanced across the seat. Holden's head lay back against the headrest, eyes closed. It seemed that the night air and the quiet ride had helped to relax him. He seemed at peace. So handsome. So, so sexy. *Mmmm.*

At that moment, she realized that all the men in her life had one common denominator: Ava.

Her lips squeezed into a hard thin line. Ava was her older brother's ex-wife, her boyfriend's assistant, and Carl Lugowski's— *Wait a minute. Carl isn't really a man in my life, right? Carl is just a friend—A friend that I sometimes turn to for help, that's all. But still, Ava is my friend's girlfriend. How much does that suck?*

On top of all of that, how Ava had managed to nab the vet assistant job still haunted her. She wanted and needed to ask Holden, but didn't feel right about it.

They parked in Holden's parking space and made their way into his apartment. The air conditioning welcomed them the moment he opened the door.

Holden Reese lived like the carefree bachelor he was. Void of any decorations, his apartment provided only the essentials: a sectional sofa, a cheap smoky glass TV stand that held a large flat screen TV. Ahhh, no self respecting bachelor could live without that. The galley kitchenette's appliances were compact-sized, including the microwave on the small counter, which was large enough for minimal baking and a quickie when an irresistible urge struck Mr. Hot Cowboy.

Holden tossed his keys onto the counter and kicked off his boots while shimming out of his sweaty T-shirt. Kate pitched her backpack onto the sofa. He flicked the T-shirt across the room to land next to her bag. Running his fingers through his tousled hair, he took a deep releasing breath as he unbuttoned his jeans.

Kate swallowed hard.

His sculpted chest, abs, and biceps always made her libido stand at attention—not to mention the spatter of hair over his chest that traveled south, encircled his navel, and trailed down to disappear below that open button of his faded jeans.

Mouthwatering.

Regardless of the distraction that his physique was stirring, she still desperately wanted to ask the question that had been burning inside her for months. The question was no longer burning. It had burst into flames. Almost involuntarily, she blurted, "Why did you hire Ava as your assistant?" *Ouch!*

Instantly, the release of stress that Holden had displayed upon entering the apartment returned to tighten its grip. His eyes narrowed. His jaw tensed, yet he said nothing. Instead, he marched down the short hallway that led to his bedroom and bathroom.

She heard the water in the shower turn on before his footsteps padded down the hall toward the kitchen. Worrying that she had overstepped her bounds, she bit her lip.

He came around the corner and grabbed her hand to escort her to the bathroom. She pulled back. He turned.

"You didn't answer my question, Holden. Why did you hire Ava?"

The water in the shower pounded against the walls. She could sense the steam billowing above the stall. He measured her, or was he measuring his answer? His gorgeous brown eyes burned into hers. His lips curled like a naughty little boy caught opening a Christmas present two days early. Pressing her up against the wall, he reached down to hook his fingers under the hem of her tank top. Slowly he inched the shirt up her torso. Never taking his eyes from hers, his fingers caressed her tummy. She quivered under the tingle of his sultry touch. His fingers crawled under the band of her bra to caress the damp skin just beneath her breasts.

He smiled.

Kissing her hard, he fisted his fingers through her hair to pull her tightly against his body. When he released the kiss, he pressed his face into her hair. "I don't want to talk, Kate," he whispered. "I want you naked in the shower. Then, I want a beer, and you naked in my bed."

Oh.

He swept her blonde locks aside to bare her throat and shoulder. With his fingers still tangled in her hair he tilted her head back to give him full access. Slowly, he smoothed his lips down her neck to taste her sweaty saltiness. Yum. Teasing, he nipped her shoulder. Purposefully, his free hand made its way to her buttocks. He squeezed to pull her against his arousal.

Oh God, her stomach clenched again. She closed her eyes. Her breathing accelerated.

He looked down at her to display an ornery smile. "Mmmm… You smell awful."

Expelling a helpless giggle, Kate opened her eyes.

"I'll have to give you a good scrubbing, Miss West, all over."

Without warning, he swept her up into his arms to make haste toward the steam billowing out of the bathroom door at the end of the hall.

His skill of distraction was most impressive.

The dirty dog. She deemed the Ava subject moot—for the time being.

Besides, it was time for a sexy cowboy shower.

Screw Ava.

The alarm clock jolted Holden from his sleep. Charlie Daniels was doing it up hot about a devil down in Georgia. The song was way over-the-top for five o'clock in the morning. Geez, morning DJ's can be really annoying. Quickly, he smacked the *OFF* button to silence Mr. Daniels fervent fiddle playing. Rubbing his eyes with the palms of his hands, he forced himself from the warm soft sheets and the warm, soft, very sexy blonde lying next to him. He looked down at Kate to find her peeking at him through half-lidded eyes.

Her hair was scattered over the pillow. Barely covering her nipples, the sheet rested across her breasts. "Good morning, Dr. Reese," she murmured in a sleepy voice.

He bent over and kissed her. "Good morning."

It was most apparent that he didn't want to go to the track and neither did Kate. She wanted him to climb back into that bed and make love to her long and hard—like he did last night.

She ran her fingers through the tuft of hair above his eyes. A smile arched her lips.

He glanced at the clock. She was most certain that he was asking himself, *Is there time for a quickie?* Not really. Even though it would be a quickie, she knew that Holden wasn't one to wane on quality. The quality of his lovemaking was off the charts.

Kate snuggled into the sheets to enjoy the view of Holden, naked, moving about the bedroom while gathering fresh underwear, T-shirt, and jeans from his dresser. His body was so beautiful. Breathing in the show, her lips curled.

He seemed lost in thought while pulling his boxer briefs onto his hips.

Her eyes narrowed when she recalled the way he had evaded her question the night before. He didn't want to answer it. *What did that insinuate?* He'd been so tense lately—irritable. She didn't want to push too hard, but she would be asking him again very soon. She had to know.

Abruptly, the blankets were swept away from her body in a *whoosh*. He stood over her. "Let's go, sleeping beauty, you're my ride, and I'm never late for work—like some people I know," he teased while admiring her breasts and the lacy pink *La Perla* panties that she was wearing.

She turned over to cover her head with the pillow. "I was only late that one time. Geez! Some people just can't let go."

After playfully swatting her rock star booty, he held out the matching pink bra between his forefinger and his thumb while sporting a salacious grin. "Get dressed. I'll make some coffee."

Peeking out from the pillow, she purred, "Mmmm, I could get used to this."

"You might not feel that way once you've tasted it."

"Uh, oh." She snatched her bra from his fingertips.

Kate could smell the coffee brewing while she washed up and put on a fresh change of clothes and a little mascara. She also heard Holden moving around the tiny kitchen. *Wonder what he's pulling together?* A smile snaked across her lips. *He's so perfect.*

When she stepped into the kitchen, a travel mug filled with steaming coffee was waiting for her on the counter. Holden was busy slathering jelly onto toasted English muffins. He looked up to flaunt his 1000 megawatt grin. "This is homemade strawberry jam. My mom sent it to me last week. She makes the best." His grin was infectious.

"Awe, fresh strawberry jam for mama's baby boy," she teased.

"You bet."

"Do your sisters ever send you anything?"

"Yeah, emails … when are you getting married? Do you have any prospects? Don't be a loser, Holden." A quiet snort escaped him at the thought of his sisters' good-natured goading.

"Mmmm, and what do you tell them?"

His smile morphed into a boyish smirk. *Irresistible.* He kissed her on the forehead. "Wouldn't you like to know."

"I asked."

"I'm pleading the fifth," he firmly stated while handing her a muffin dripping with jam.

"You mean like you did last night?" She shyly peeked at him through her lashes.

His grin disappeared along with her confidence in the probe. His gaze turned icy and his face hardened. He muttered, "Please, Kate, let it go."

She searched the floor for the confidence that had fallen and shattered into pieces. "I need to know, Holden. I really do. Why?" Her words fell away to a whisper.

His jaw clenched. He leaned a hip against the counter and crossed his arms over his chest. He had to know that this wasn't going to go away. After a moment, he said, "I asked you first.

You said no. Ava came to see me. She had very good credentials. I hired her because I needed an assistant. Okay? Can we drop it now?" His tone was thick with warning. The carefree, fun-loving Holden that she woke to this morning had been swapped with the irritable, hesitant Holden who surfaced more often than not lately.

She decided upon a quick rebuttal. "What if I said yes? What if I said that I would come to work for you now?" She couldn't believe the words tumbling from her lips. Was she really willing to leave Doc Spears? *Cripes. What was all that about?*

Holden was clearly taken aback. She could see that he didn't know how to respond. "Ahhh…um…that wouldn't be very fair to Ava."

"So?"

"I don't want to be a prick, Kate."

"I understand. How about if I talk to Ben and see if he's willing to make a switch?" Now she was really shocked by her own words.

She had to be bluffing because Ben Spears would never agree to it. He was totally pissed when Ava gave her abrupt notice.

She watched Holden fidget and twitch like he was waiting to be rescued from a burning house, or maybe he was praying for divine intervention. Was he really that worried about Ava's feelings? Why?

Holden's stomach twisted into the tight knot that had taken up residence over the past weeks. Suddenly, his mom's homemade jam didn't look quite so appetizing. He tramped down hard on the trash can lever to open the lid, pitched the muffin into the can, and then stomped toward the door.

"We're going to be late."

~ Four ~

Eric was stunned.

Punch was tongue-tied.

Eugene was exasperated. His second day at Westwood didn't seem to be going any better than the first.

Eric's face was red and looked redder compared to the white fencing of the paddock behind the barn. It was quite obvious that his blood pressure was on the rise. "How in God's name did you lose my prize broodmare between the paddock and the barn door?" he asked in a low voice.

It truly was amazing because there was no more than twenty feet between the barn door and the paddock where Eugene was taking Tejan in order for Punch to rasp her hooves. The fat broodmare was now nowhere in sight.

"Well…yes, sir," Eugene stammered. "I'm very sorry. She—"

"Look, Eric, Eugene's new at handling horses. It's my fault. I shouldn't have let him lead her." Punch scanned the area in hopes that she would appear out of nowhere. No luck.

"Tejan's as gentle as a kitten!" Eric yelled.

"Yes, sir, she sure is, but I musta brought my hand up to pet her face a little too quick. She just pulled back, and I wasn't ready—"

Eugene began to explain before Punch grabbed him by the arm to drag him toward the wooded area behind the barn.

"Don't worry about it, Eric," Punch said. "We'll find her right away."

Eric stepped in front of them. "No way! I'm not going to have the two of you chasing my most expensive broodmare into Rosemount!" He slid into the ATV that was parked outside the paddock gate. "I'll find her myself!" The ATV spit dirt into the air when it flew around the paddock fence.

Punch pursed his lips in agitation. Eugene hung his head. They looked like two boys who had been scolded for not white washing a fence properly: Tom Sawyer and Huckleberry Finn.

"This ain't working out, Punch," Eugene said. "Everything I touch goes to shit."

Punch pressed his lips into a thin line. "Take it easy, Eugene. It's your first week on the job. You're bound to make a few mistakes. You'll get the hang of it." He slapped Eugene on the back. "C'mon, we've got plenty of work waiting for us at the broodmare shed."

Punch turned to find Charlatan walking out the barn with Sheldon close behind. Shaking his head, Punch planted his hands on his hips. "What are you doing out here, Charlie?" He reached into his hip pocket and pulled out a peppermint.

Charlatan's ears immediately flipped up, his top lip curled up over his big nostrils.

Sheldon found the sound of the paper crinkling most interesting, too. Arching his neck, he snorted, and hid behind Charlatan to cautiously gauge what the peppermint was all about.

Punch stroked Charlatan's head while he slipped the peppermint into his mouth. He then unwrapped another for Sheldon. He held the mint in his calloused hand while slowly extending it toward the nervous youngster.

Sheldon's nostrils flared. Apprehensively, he stretched his neck and then snatched the mint from the hand.

"Are you teaching Sheldon your wicked ways?" he asked the big grey gelding.

Charlatan snorted.

"I thought so." Chuckling, he took the horse by his halter. "C'mon, we'd better get you two in the paddock before Mike finds out."

"Do you want me to lead Sheldon?" Eugene reached for the colt's halter.

"No!" Punch panicked, and then softened his tone. "Er, no need, I think he'll just follow along behind Charlie."

The morning workouts had come to an end. The racetrack was now closed so that the track crew could prepare for the evening races.

Other than *"Good morning,"* Holden hadn't said one word to Ava. When they were in stables, he would talk around her to the trainer or the stable hands. When he needed something from her, he would tell her what he needed without so much as a glance in her direction.

It was unnerving. Ava wasn't used to hostility from a man—even passive hostility. Men were usually eating out of her hand and wanting more. Holden's derision for her was quite concise and most unsettling.

Except for his hostility, Holden seemed a little less tense. She was guessing that it was because they didn't visit Chip's stable. She was feeling relieved herself.

She glanced at the clock on the dashboard. Yep, it was almost time to quit for the afternoon. They would return for pre-race rounds at four o'clock. Sitting patiently in the truck, she waited for Holden to finish giving an exercise rider instruction for her pony's cough when the cell phone rang. She reached into the cup holder to retrieve the phone, "Reese vet services…"

"Well, hello, angel, how's my girl today?" Chip's scandalous tone seeped into her ear.

She took a deep apprehensive breath. Chip Walker did something to her that no other man ever did: He scared her. The man was handsome. He was someone that she would usually be attracted to. For some reason she couldn't figure out, he made her skin crawl.

"I'm fine, thank you." She clipped off each word. With a wave of her hand, she caught Holden's attention through the windshield and gestured to him that he had a call. "Would like to talk with Dr. Reese?"

"If I have to…"

"You do," she told him in a curt tone. She handed Holden the phone when he opened door. "It's Chip."

Holden snatched the phone from her and pressed it against his chest. "Don't answer my cell phone, Ava!"

"It's the vet assistant's job," she replied. She was shocked at yet another change in protocol. How was she supposed to keep up?

"Not anymore!" He slammed the truck door and dragged in a terse breath before lifting the phone to his face. "What's up, Chip?"

"I need more. We've got a new client," Chip said in a casual tone.

"*We* don't have clients, *you* do," Holden said through clenched teeth. "I don't want to be involved any further. You got that?" He looked around the shed row while speaking as covertly as possible out in the open.

"I like you, Doc. Don't make me destroy you. You've got it all: a growing practice, good looks, and beautiful women all around you. I have the power to take it all away. *Have you got that?*"

Holden didn't respond.

Chip liked that. "I'll expect you in fifteen minutes."

The connection went dead.

Holden felt like both Ava and Chip owned a piece of him; a very dark slice of his soul that he had no idea had been up for grabs.

Chip was right, he could lose it all: his practice, his freedom, and Kate. Losing his freedom and his livelihood would be a disaster. Losing Kate would be unbearable.

He climbed into the truck, ran a hand through his hair, and tossed his phone into the cup holder.

"Talk to me, Holden," Ava whispered from across the cab. There was sincerity in her voice—sweet concern.

"You are the last person I would talk to, Ava," he said through a clenched jaw.

Ava bit her lip. She could see the struggle on his face. He was angry and troubled. She was actually feeling a tug of compassion for him. He looked lost and desperate. He reminded her of her boyfriend Carl. Holden was basically a good guy, except he'd got himself tangled up with Chip in some dangerous circumstance. *Big mistake.*

"I want us to be friends—" she said.

"Friends don't blackmail friends, Ava."

"I'm not blackmailing you, Holden—"

"What would you call it?"

"Job security." Ava squeezed her laced fingers tightly on her lap.

"Blackmail."

"It's not totally my fault, you know. You didn't have to have sex with me in your bed, and the shower, and on the kitchen counter."

Holden dropped his head against the headrest hard and squeezed his eyes closed. He attempted to take in a calming breath. He said, "I made a mistake. That said I know how we can fix it, and you will still have plenty of job security."

Ava raised her eyebrow, crossed her arms under her breasts and dragged her gaze to meet his. "Do you now? What are you suggesting, Dr. Reese?"

Her tone was laconic. Not a good sign. He swallowed hard before he began. "A switch. You go back to work for Doc Spears, and Kate would come to work for me."

Her eyes widened. Her nostrils flared.

He braced himself.

"How can I say this so that you will completely understand? No!"

"Blackmail," he said in a low, menacing tone. "Pure and simple."

"Whatever, Dr. Reese." She shouldered the truck door open and slid from the seat. "I'll see you at four o'clock."

He watched her strut down the shed row toward the parking lot. Gliding her fingers through her long auburn hair, she was a woman that most men had a hard desire for—not Holden. He found her heartless, self-absorbed in her beauty and her insatiable need to control men. He hadn't spent a lot of time with Mike West, but he couldn't figure how he could've been in love with such a manipulating witch.

The tension and anger, at himself, at Ava, and at Chip Walker was like a scorching acid drip through his veins.

He looked down at the clock on the dashboard. Five minutes until he was to be at Walker stables.

He punched the steering wheel.

❧ ❧ ❧ ❧

Sighing, Kate glanced across the cab of Doc Spears' vet truck. Doc's jutted lip signified his deep concentration while studying the list of horses they would inject with lassix during pre-race rounds later.

He was in the habit of memorizing the list, *"to keep my mind sharp,"* he would explain. Evidently the simple exercise was working. The old vet was as spry as the day was long…and hot…and tiring. Kate was always amazed at how the sixty-eight-year-old man with pure white hair remembered everything. For crying-out-loud, he would have to remind her of stable calls they were responsible for, or an appointment she needed to keep at the end of the day. Oh yes, Dr. Ben Spears had his act together. There was no getting one over on him.

She bit her lip while fiddling with the clip of the vet box in her lap. Her conversation with Holden that morning kept running through her head. When he had offered her the vet assistant position several months ago, she didn't feel that their relationship was ready for the constant togetherness that working for him would present.

Unconsciously, she rolled her eyes at herself. Holden was right, he did ask her first, and she did turn him down. *C'mon, how could I possibly have known that Ava would pounce at the job?* She had upset Holden with her questions. His moods were so unpredictable. *Does it have something to do with Ava?* Nevertheless, he seemed to want to protect her. *What's that about?*

The clip on the box flicked to prick her finger. Flinching, she drew her finger to her mouth. She peeked at Doc Spears. *Do I dare ask him to switch for Ava? Are Holden and I ready for constant togetherness? Could our relationship survive with Ava in the middle?*

The truth was that her blood boiled every time she saw Ava in Holden's truck. She had to hold herself back from scratching Ava's eyes out. *So seventh grade.*

Visions of Ava and Holden between satin sheets, her naked body wrapped around his often invaded her thoughts. It was her imagination running amuck, yet the visions were hard to shake, and even harder to ignore. She never considered herself a jealous woman. Dr. Holden Reese was her man. Ava West wasn't going to get a piece of him. Not in this lifetime!

Doc Spears didn't look up from his list when he asked, "Something you want to talk to me about?"

Kate was taken aback. "How do you do that?"

"Fidgety women always want to talk. You're fidgety." He turned to her with an impassive expression. "What's on your mind, West?"

"I can't stand Ava working with Holden," she out-right confessed.

"I kinda figured."

She drew in a braced breath. "I want to work with Holden, Ben." She could feel the unwelcome flush on her cheeks. Embarrassed, she looked down at the clip on her box. "I'm in love with him…" Her voice fell away.

"And…"

"And…I was hoping that you'd agree to take Ava back so I could go to Holden. As much as I despise her, I have to admit she's an excellent vet assistant. You know that as well as I, and…"

"And you wouldn't have to worry about Ava getting her hands on Holden."

The flush on her cheeks burned more brilliantly. Her cheeks were blazing. She murmured, "Something like that."

Dropping his chin into his chest, Doc Spears pursed his lips. "You're sure that this is what you want?"

Was it? Was it what she really wanted? It was a huge step. She hoped that it was the right step, but was it for the right reasons? Tears came to her eyes.

Doc Spears could see the torment in her posture.

For several years, Ava had worked for him before Kate came along. Over that time, he had watched Ava work over quite a few men—including Kate's brother. Understanding where Kate was coming from, he took in a deep breath. "Well young lady, as much as I'd miss you, I'm not one to get in the way of true love. If this is what you want, and if Ava is agreeable, I'll go along with it."

Wiping a tear away with the back of her hand, she choked out. "Thank you, Ben."

❧ ❧ ❧ ❧

After the morning workouts, the backside of Keystone Downs would empty out as if someone had screamed *"hurricane a comin'."* The shed rows would become like a ghost town. Steam from fresh horse dung in the rusted manure bins in the middle of the road-ways would rise like wicked phantoms into the oncoming heat of the day. The pigeons perched on the roofs of the stables would peer down upon the barn cats lazily sunning themselves. The only sound would be the echo of the constant rumble of the John Deere tractors harrowing the racetrack.

Rubbing his temples, Holden sat in his truck outside Chip's stable. With an aggravated groan, he slid from the truck to make his way into the stable. He was ten minutes late.

The sound of Chip's voice made him flinch when he slipped through the door. "Hey! There he is! Theeee man!" While slapping him hard on the back, Chip grabbed Holden's hand to shake it. "Tell me, dude, which is better? The blonde or the redhead?"

Holden's eyes narrowed into a glare.

Chip's mouth opened to a wide "O". He pointed at him wearing a scandalous grin. Lowering his voice to a high-pitched whisper, he screeched, "Oh my God! You're doin' them at the same time? You lucky-ass bastard!"

"Fuck-off, Chip," Holden bit out.

"I would love to, mainly with the redhead, but if you can spare the blonde—"

Holden grabbed him by the shirt. The right corner of Chip's lip curled. Seeing that Holden was in no mood for his dirty sarcasm, Chip raised his hands in surrender and changed course. "On second thought, my sources tell me that you and the blonde are a thing."

Seething, Holden released Chip's shirt and shoved his hands into the pockets of his jeans. He was terrified of what he might do with them otherwise.

With an arched brow, Chip went into his office. Holden followed.

They were almost to the threshold when Chip's cell phone rang. Glancing at the screen, he pressed the button with a scowl. Raising the phone to his ear, he said, "Give me some good news."

Holden could tell by the twist of aggravation on Chip's face that the poor schmuck on the other end was not fulfilling his request.

"Keep looking," Chip ordered. "He's in the area. Send someone into Rosemount for a look. Don't call again until you've spotted him." He pressed the *STOP* button sucked in a cleansing breath, and stepped into the office.

Chip's stable office was unlike any of the others at Keystone Downs. Even the prominent stables, like Westwood, didn't furnish their offices with such chic décor. The walls in Chip's office were covered in fine cherry paneling. Pictures of his racing victories hung in neat rows adorned in gold frames.

Chip opened a drawer in the lovely black lacquer desk and retrieved two piles of banded bills. With an ear-to-ear smile, he held the money out to Holden. "This should brighten your mood, Doc. Ten thousand big ones. You've made a huge difference in people's lives. Horses that weren't good for nothing anymore are winning, and we're collecting twenty percent of the purse from each trainer that's participating in our program."

"Your program, Chip. I'm out. Keep your freakin' money. I'll keep my mouth shut, but I'm out. Find someone else."

Chip dropped the money onto the desk. A wicked scowl slithered across his face. "The blonde. Isn't she a West? Hmmm, don't think that bunch would be too happy to find out what you are—a low-life hit-an-run driver." He moved in closer.

Holden's jaw clenched.

Chip could smell his apprehension. He owned the young vet, and he knew it. "Don't think I've forgotten about what happened six months ago on Warriors Road. I was right behind you when you came out of the bar. You were pretty fucked-up. You shouldn't have been driving and when you ran that girl over, I couldn't believe it. But ya know what I couldn't get over?" He moved closer to Holden's face, "The way you drove off and just left her layin' there. Ahhh, I understand. The lawsuits, losing your vet license, it was a no-win situation for sure. Good thing I'm quick on my feet. No one saw but me, and so when I told the cop that the hit and run was driving a blue Ford pickup instead of your vet truck, they never came looking for you, did they?"

Holden pushed Chip away. "No, but you did. And I gave you exactly what you asked for in exchange for your silence. You said it was a one-time deal. That you'd forget you ever saw the accident, but you just keep coming back for more. I didn't mean to hit her. I wasn't drunk. I was tired—that's all. Maybe I had one drink too many. Thing is—I fell asleep. Besides—The girl didn't die. So why don't you leave me the hell alone?"

"It don't matter, Doc. I have a feelin' that pretty blonde and her rich-ass family won't be none too forgiving. Hey, you haven't made out too bad. You've made a shit load of money, too. If I go to the police, your ass will be in jail for a long time to come." He watched Holden wipe the sweat from his brow.

"Listen up. We've got a real sweet deal goin' on, Doc. You do your part, my buddy at the pharmacy does his, and my brother in the test barn makes sure they don't test for certain drugs on certain days."

Seeing Holden's surprise with this news, Chip revealed. "Yep, Tony in the test barn is my half-brother. Mom married his day a couple years ago. We treat each other like strangers, and no one's the wiser. Everyone's making a tidy profit. So, unless you want me to blow your world apart, you'll do what you're told and take the goddamned money." He shoved the bundles into Holden's chest so hard that he knocked him backward. Chip added, "Right. Now."

❧ ☙ ❧ ❧

Like most evenings, Punch was the last to leave. He liked to walk the barn's aisles one more time to make sure all the horses were quiet. His thoughts drifted to the man that he found teetering at the edge of the bridge two days ago. Even though Eugene had a few mishaps in the past days, he seemed to be at ease with his work at the broodmare shed and happy to have his hands busy working toward an end result.

Eugene still hadn't confided to Punch about what had brought him to such a low place, and Punch hadn't asked. Was it a woman? Debt? Or did the man have himself tangled up in something more sinister? Eugene showed no signs of drug or alcohol abuse. In fact, he was very athletic, well-muscled—like someone who worked out hard on a daily basis. It would be naive to rule out the possibility that Eugene's problems were connected to a drug deal gone sideways. Maybe as time passed, Eugene would trust Punch enough to unburden himself. Maybe.

When he swatted at the light switch to darken the barn, Punch heard a shuffle, and a rake smack against the floor. Punch had his suspicions about who was making the ruckus. Dang, the least Charlatan could do was wait until the barn was closed up and the lights were off. The talented escape artist was becoming cocky. It was as if he didn't give two shits who was around when he managed his break-out.

Sure enough, when Punch turned, the imposing grey gelding stood in the aisle nuzzling the latch on Sheldon's stall until it bumped and banged and finally popped open. Punch crossed his arms over his chest. Maybe it was time for Charlatan to find a new vocation. He needed something else to focus on. The Thoroughbred refused to race. *Okay, so now's a good time to show him another way.*

Punch wandered down the barn aisle toward Charlatan who was now pushing Sheldon's stall door open far enough for the youngster to squeeze through. Punch slammed the door closed. Sheldon jumped back into the stall. Charlatan's head jerked up, his eyes wide, and his nostrils flared. He expelled an indignant snort. He looked most affronted.

"I think it's time to put that extra energy of yours to better use, dude," Punch said.

Knowing that his good buddy always kept peppermints, Charlatan nuzzled his pocket.

"You are a charmer, aren't you?" Punch said. "C'mon." He took the gelding by the halter and led him back to his stall, only instead of closing the door and attaching the latch, he clipped the horse's halter to a tie-up. He patted Charlatan's neck. "Now don't go anywhere. I'll be right back."

Charlatan was disappointed that Punch did not toss a peppermint in his direction. He impatiently pawed at the sawdust on the floor while watching Punch mosey down the aisle where he disappeared into the tack room. A few moments later, he emerged carrying a western saddle, pad, and a bridle.

This looked serious.

Charlatan's ears perked. He stopped pawing.

Punch slid the stall door open, dropped the saddle, and then stroked Charlatan's neck again. He tossed the pad over his back, and then placed the saddle on the pad. With ease, he secured the girth. He removed Charlatan's halter, slipped the bit into his mouth, pulled the headstall over his head, and then connected the throat latch.

Punch was a huge man, but Charlatan was a big sturdy Thoroughbred. He wasn't small boned or dainty. His legs were stout and his chest and rump were wide and muscled.

They weren't going for a sprint; they were going for a nice slow moonlit trail ride.

Punch wanted Charlatan to relax and enjoy the ride. "C'mon, big guy, let's see if we can't make an honest horse out of you yet." He led Charlatan from the stall, shoved his foot in the stirrup, hoisted his body up, and threw his leg over the saddle. After settling in the saddle, he urged the gelding forward down the aisle.

A smile snaked across his lips as he remembered his old buddy, Cody, the old Quarter Horse who he rode for many years.

It had been only six months ago since his old friend was injured while running down an out-of-control mare on the training track. Now retired, the ole boy lived among the broodmares. Punch missed Cody. He missed sitting in the saddle.

The leather beneath him squeaked as the horse clopped along.

He steered Charlatan along the trail that led to the training track. The purple haze of dusk draped the sky, and the stars twinkled between the tangles of branches overhead. Charlatan seemed at ease walking along the dirt road. The training track yawned before them in the night shadows. Charlatan headed straight for the opening, yet Punch did not urge him through the gate onto the track. The horse's ears perked straight up and his nostrils flared. He was anticipating a good gallop in the sand. Instead, Punch reined the horse around the perimeter of the race rail and guided him into the tall grasses.

Charlatan settled into the slow easy pace.

The crickets sang and the half-moon lazily climbed into the sky above the tree tops.

Punch used to take Cody for moonlight rides. It was tranquil to be among the shadowy beauty that Mother Nature offered in the moonlight.

~ FIVE ~

Eugene was feeling pretty confident by his third day at the farm. It was eleven o'clock in the morning and he hadn't been involved in or caused a debacle. Hey, so far, so good.

He had spent the entire morning working with Punch in the broodmare shed. Finishing up the preliminary work on the wall that had to be done before the blocks could be laid, he was in his element: laying blocks, working with his hands, or fighting with his fists.

Thoroughbreds? Not so much.

On the hill overlooking the beautiful rolling landscape of Westwood, the shed was a much safer environment. It offered fewer opportunities to get into trouble.

Eugene hadn't told Punch about his violent occupation. It wouldn't be necessary since he didn't plan on hanging around for very long. When the time was right, he'd be on the move.

He floated the last bit of water from the cement away from the footer that they had to build. He was thankful that it was almost ready for the block work to begin.

Beads of sweat dribbled down his back. The heat was pounding down upon them.

Punch handed him a bottle of water at the same time that the phone in his hip pocket rang. "Yeah," he said into his cell. "No problem, I'll be right there." He stuffed the phone back into his pocket. After taking a long gulp of water, he told Eugene, "Eric's still in some meeting so Mike needs our help at the racetrack. C'mon, it'll be a nice break." Punch gulped down the rest of the water while walking toward the Gator. When he reached the vehicle, he realized Eugene wasn't following him. He turned to find him looking at his feet. "Aren't you coming?"

Eugene seemed to be weighing his options. Finally, he said, "Naw, I think the racetrack would be a bad idea. If it's all the same to you, think I'll just stay here. Didn't you say there were some boards that needed to be moved?"

Punch shrugged. "Suit yourself. There's a pile of eight-by-tens in the equine swimming facility that need moved up here. If you're sure you don't want to come along …"

"I'll take care of the boards. Catch ya later."

Punch slid into the Gator. "Fair enough."

Movement in the sky caught his eye. "Hey, there she is!" He grabbed the binoculars from the seat.

The red-tailed hawk thrust her claws forward while flailing her broad wings to land on the nest.

"She's got a rabbit for the little ones," Punch said.

Struggling to see in the bright sunshine, Eugene cupped his hands over his forehead.

Punch handed him the binoculars.

"I'll be damned," Eugene muttered. "Wonder when she'll teach them to fly?"

Punch let out a laugh. "Probably when we're not watching. Nature doesn't always appreciate spectators." When Eugene tried to hand him the binoculars, he said, "Let's just keep them in the barn."

Eugene watched the Gator disappear over the hill before he made his way back into the barn.

Searching the small stable, he laid the binoculars aside. He made note of the kick boards that lined each of the stalls. Quickly, he grabbed a hammer and, with the claw-end, he pried the heavy nails from the thick oak boards until he loosened one.

The space between the kick board and the wall was about six inches wide. It was clogged with spider webs and hayseed and dirt, but it was a space nonetheless.

The left side of Eugene's mouth lifted. He pounded the board back into place, only not quite as tightly as it had originally been secured.

◦§ ◦◦ ◦§ ◦◦

The water lapped against the wall of the equine swimming pool. The pungent smell of chlorine filled the muggy air. The sun beat through the arched windows that surrounded the perimeter of the facility.

Shane yanked his T-shirt over his head and tossed it aside. It was too hot for a shirt today. Making sure that his MP-3 player was securely in the pocket of his jeans, he pressed the ear buds into his ears. His lips curled and his head bobbed to the beat when he picked up the vacuum to clean the pool. Cleaning the pool was a tedious job, but listening to some cool tunes made it a little more tolerable.

Slowly, he walked around the rim while sweeping the vacuum back and forth over the floor of the pool. The vacuum's steady *whirr* and the music filled his ears. Soon, he joined in to hum along.

Whistling a tune, Eugene made his way into the equine swimming area and spotted the pile of boards stacked against the far wall like Punch had said they would be. Noticing the youngest West working the vacuum over the pool, he called out, "Hey, Shane."

With his back to Eugene, his mind on the vacuum, and the music from his MP-3 player, Shane gave no response.

"Hot as hell, ain't it?" Eugene said.

Yet again Shane didn't respond.

Shrugging, Eugene shot him a curious look. Either the kid was stand-offish or hard of hearing. It didn't matter. He came to do a job.

Eyeing up the pile of boards, he realized that it would be wise to make sure Shane knew he was going to move them. The last thing he wanted was to whack the kid with a board and knock him into the pool. Day Three was going well—no need to screw it up.

When he approached Shane, Eugene realized why the young man hadn't responded to his conversation—he didn't hear him with the music playing in his ears. Chuckling, he tapped Shane firmly on the shoulder. "Hey!"

Shane flinched. His feet slipped over the wet edge of the pool. His arms flailed. Eugene managed to grab him by the shoulders to steady him.

Tossing him an annoyed look, Shane pulled the buds from his ears. "What's up?"

"I'm here for the boards. I just wanted you to know that I'm behind you."

"Thanks," Shane said.

Eugene gestured toward the equine swimming pool. "All of this kind of reminds me when I used to clean the pool at the governor's mansion. He had a pool *just* like this one."

Shane lifted his chin. His eyes narrowed as he looked down at the equine pool. The sides of the pool were curved inward so that the horses could not climb out of the pool. At the far end was a ramp with a bridge that lowered over the opening to block yet another escape route, and so that the person leading the horse during the swim could walk across the ramp. He questioned the accuracy of Eugene's statement. "I can't believe that the governor has a pool just like this one."

Grinning, Eugene slapped him hard on the back.

Not expecting the jolt, Shane crashed into the pool.

Gasping for the air that had been stolen from him, Shane surfaced quickly while wiping the sting of chlorine from his eyes. Panicked, he yanked the MP-3 player from his pocket. It was drenched. The music had silenced. Thoroughly disgusted, he tossed Eugene a dirty look while launching the gadget out of the pool.

"Why is it always me that ends up in the damned horse water?!" he yelled.

Even though Shane was wet and pissed about losing his MP-3 player, he let Eugene use the farm truck to transfer the boards to the broodmare shed. The kid waved his hand at him while marching out of the pool area when Eugene asked if he could use the truck to go to the local Stop and Shop convenience store for some soda pop and bread.

After he had finished transferring the boards to the broodmare shed, he climbed into the old Ford and drove down the dirt road, along the winding driveway, and out onto Ridge Road. He drove for two miles before he came to the place where Reardon's Run Road intersected with Ridge. He made the right turn onto Reardon's Run Road instead of continuing further along Ridge toward the Stop and Shop.

Finally, he arrived at the tree where he had wrecked his car. He parked the truck alongside the road. The roar of the water thrashing in Reardon's Run wafted through the open driver's side window. Slowly, he slid out of the truck. Scanning the area, he made his way through the high weeds toward the barricaded entrance to the old bridge. He peered over the barricade at the long length of old rusted rails that lay over warped and splintered planking. The water whipping over the rocks far below the bridge was much louder at the barricade. Stealthily, he looked around, and then climbed over the barrier to make his way past the huge hole in the planking where Punch had fallen through until he reached the railing.

He clutched the railing with a white knuckle grip while staring down into the white waters below. Swirling white caps made his head spin and his stomach tighten. Taking in a deep gulp of air, he lifted his foot but came to an abrupt halt when he heard, "Eugene!" He spun to find Eric West making the same careful trek across the bridge toward him.

"I wasn't gonna jump, Mr. West," Eugene told him.

Eric gauged him with a tight stare. "What're you doing here?"

"I... um... lost my cell phone when I was here the other day. Thought I'd come to see if I could find it. Shane said I could use the truck." Eugene took in Eric's untrusting gaze. "It sure is a long way down there. I'm thankful neither Punch nor I ended up in the creek the other day."

"Did you find your phone?" Eric asked.

"No," Eugene muttered, "maybe it's in the water."

"I think we should get back to the farm," Eric said in a tone that told Eugene there wasn't another option.

∽ ∂ ∽ ℘

The lunch crowd had poured into the cafeteria at Keystone Downs. Their morning gallop fees at stake, several exercise riders were engrossed in their usual lunchtime poker game at the table at the far end of the cafeteria.

Waiting for their sandwich orders from the bar, the trainers paced back and forth while talking into their cell phones.

As always, four old retired jockeys took it all in at a corner table while sucking on their cigarettes with their craggy lips. Doc Spears pressed through the doors and took a seat with the old jocks to spin yarns of the days when Keystone Downs ran tough races—in their opinion anyway. Taking his seat, he noticed Ava carrying a tray with a turkey sandwich to a table across the room. He dreaded the thought of losing Kate to take Ava back into his employ. Nonetheless, Kate was right; Ava was an excellent vet assistant. She knew her stuff and was as efficient as anyone he knew. It was only her manipulative demeanor that put him off. He was glad when she had resigned—only to be returning way too soon.

Wonder how she feels about the arrangement? He couldn't imagine that she would be freely agreeable. She was too happy to turn in her notice. Whatever the circumstances they conjured up, he would abide for the sake of Kate's happiness.

Ava settled into a seat and was about to take the first bite of her sandwich when two strong hands clasped her shoulders. The fingers dug deep into her muscles to knead them firmly. With her mouth wrapped around the bun, Ava froze. Her eyes widened. The hands soon smoothed over her shoulders and caressed them tenderly while making their way down her arms.

Lowering his face into her hair, Chip whispered into her ear, "Feel good, angel? Imagine what else I can do with my hands."

Stiffening, she inhaled—unable to exhale. She dropped the sandwich onto the plate. "Please take your hands off of me," she said through gritted teeth.

Tightening his grip, Chip nibbled at her ear. With a sultry voice from deep in his throat, he cajoled, "C'mon baby, we have all afternoon to get to know each other real well. Don't play hard-to-get. That's no fun at all."

"Not in this lifetime. Now take your hands off of me, Mr. Walker," Ava wiggled away from his grasp.

"I know you're giving it to Reese and I can tell you've got plenty to spare. C'mon, angel, give it up," he said a bit louder.

Unable to stand it, she spun in her seat and slapped him across the face.

Chip jerked back. Recovering quickly, he grabbed her wrist and smiled. "I figured you liked it rough. We can do that, too."

"She doesn't want you touching her, Chip. So back-off!" Holden's voice was terse and uncompromising.

Chip slowly released Ava's arm and turned toward the tall, hard-bodied man standing behind him.

A blanket of silence fell over the cafeteria. The two men stared at each other while waiting for the other to blink or throw a punch.

The skin over Holden's jaw was so tight that it rippled over the bone. His eyes seethed.

A slow deliberate grin crept across Chip's face. Glancing over Holden's shoulder, he raised his hands in surrender. He spat out a playful snort. "Like I said, Doc, you've got the best of both worlds: redhead by day, blonde by night." With that, Chip shouldered past him to saunter toward the cafeteria door that Kate had just walked through.

Her mouth hung slightly open. Her eyes were wide with misgiving and her nostrils flared in agitation.

Holden's gaze met Kate's. His brown guilty eyes met her blue eyes which were burning with suspicion.

The world seemed to come to a jolting stop.

They stood staring at each other. Holden said nothing. Kate could feel all eyes in the cafeteria on her as the red flush of agitation skittered up her neck and into her cheeks. Again, Holden was defending Ava. Only this time it was a public display of fortification. Curling her hands into tight fists, Kate turned and marched out of the cafeteria.

Holden raked his fingers through his hair. He didn't know what to say or do. He felt the need to chase after her to explain, except he thought that would only perpetuate a scene. *Perhaps it's best to let her cool off for a while.* He could only imagine all the wrong things coming out of his mouth. *Perhaps distance is the best remedy for now.*

⁊ ⁊ ⁊ ⁊

Lying in bed, staring at the ceiling fan whirling round and round over her, Kate reasoned with herself. When she had stomped out of the cafeteria, her blood was at the boiling point. *Why was Holden protecting Ava?*

To top it all off, Chip's words, *"Like I said, Doc, you've got the best of both worlds: redhead by day, blonde by night,"* played over and over in her mind. What did that mean? The scene in the cafeteria made for a long afternoon, and an even longer evening at the racetrack while trudging from stable to stable with Doc Spears. She felt like her head would surely explode. When they would pass Holden's truck with Ava in the passenger's seat, animosity chased through her gut like she'd never felt before. Pure disdain.

Holden caught up with her when she was getting ready to leave the track for the night. He pressed her to come to his apartment to talk things through, but she couldn't. She needed to get it all straight in her head before she could set it straight with him.

He had evaded her questions about Ava only a night ago. *Something's up.* Her mother used to often recite the old cliché: *Where there's smoke, there's fire.*

She spent the afternoon and evening wondering what kind of fire Ava had lit under her cowboy, her lover, and the man she wanted to be with more than anything in this world.

Lying in her bed alone in the dark and the quiet, regret came to clench her every breath. *Wouldn't I want someone to come to my defense if a creep like Chip Walker was pawing me? Wouldn't I want Carl Lugowski to tell him to back-off if he was standing nearby? As a matter of fact, Carl has come to my aide on several occasions. I called him, and he came—Ava's lover came. So why does it make me so angry that Holden stepped in when Ava was in a bind?*

The answer was simple: because it was Ava. Period.

Jesus.

Tears pricked her eyes. She had no right to be angry with Holden. He was doing what any gentleman would do: fend-off a sexual predator. Ironically, Ava was usually said predator. In this instance she was the victim. It was hard to picture Ava as a victim, but indeed, that's exactly what she was. She did not desire Chip's advances. For some reason Chip Walker's penis wasn't on Ava's wish list. Go figure. Regardless, Holden was simply doing what he thought was right: defending a woman. Not necessarily Ava, any woman in that position. That was the kind of man her cowboy was—honorable.

Idiot.

Squeezing her eyes closed, tears burned the rim of her lids. Kate ran her fingers through her hair. A miserable sob escaped from her throat. Regret opened the door to invite shame to envelope her with swift efficiency. She had to tell Holden how sorry she was, how irrational she had been. Urgency overwhelmed her. She needed to tell him now. She turned to the alarm clock on her night stand: one o'clock in the morning. *No matter, it had to be now. Right now.*

❧ ❧ ❧ ❧

Holden tossed in his bed. There would be no sleep tonight. He flopped onto his back. He couldn't stand-by and let Chip grope Ava. It wasn't right. It seemed that everything in his life wasn't right—except his relationship with Kate. Most of it, Holden couldn't do anything about—unless he was willing to endure the fall-out. Damn it, making unwelcome advances at a woman was something that he could put a stop to—even if the woman was Ava. So he did. Hopefully, Kate would figure that out.

Lacing his fingers together, he covered his eyes. The sudden sound of pounding brought him bolting upward to his elbows. Cocking his head, he listened. Someone was knocking at his door. He glanced at the clock on his night stand: one-forty-five in the morning. Slowly, he slid from the bed, snatched his jeans from the floor, stepped into them, and slid them up his hips.

The knocking continued.

Running his hand through his bed-tousled hair, he padded down the hallway and flicked on the kitchen light as he past. Rocked by irritation, he twisted the deadbolt and yanked open the door with a *whoosh*.

Shock, followed by relief, washed over him when he found Kate peering up at him—her blue watery eyes gazing into his brown hopeful ones.

Kate flung her arms around him, buried her face into his chest and breathed in his scent while kissing his skin. "I'm so sorry, Holden," she muttered into his torso.

He folded her into his arms, laid his cheek on the top of her head, and gently rocked her back and forth in his embrace. "You're my only girl, Kate." His fingers found her chin. He lifted her face to look into her eyes. "But I couldn't let Walker harass Ava like that. It wouldn't be right, Kate. You've got to know that."

Shame danced a jig on her right shoulder, while regret merrily jumped up and down on her left.

Holden ran the pad of his thumb across her cheek. The one thing he hadn't screwed up in his life was standing in front of him.

"I know," Kate whispered. "But when I saw you defending her something in my head popped. I guess I flew off the handle. I'm sorry. Forgive me?"

The corners of Holden's mouth lifted. He eased Kate through the door. After closing it behind her, he pressed her against it. Imprisoning her between his arms, he leaned forward until his nose was almost touching hers. "That depends, Miss West, is there make-up sex involved in this forgiveness you're asking for?"

She matched his spicy smirk. "Aren't we overconfident?"

His eyes widened at the challenge. "This from a woman who showed up on my doorstep dressed in her jammies?"

Remembering that she was wearing a white cami, powder blue satin pajama pants, and a pair of flip-flops, her cheeks warmed.

Straightening, Holden said, "Let's try something. Put your hands over your head for a moment."

Unsure what he was getting at, she did as he asked.

Quickly, he took hold of the hem of her cami, slipped it over her head, and tossed it to the floor. He breathed in deep at the sight of her round plump breasts bobbing back into place. Instantly, her dusty pink nipples stiffened—super-sensitized by his hungry gaze.

"That's better, now how about these pants?" He hooked his fingers over the waistband of her pants and her panties. Taking no prisoners, he slid them to her knees. Pausing, he raised his eyebrows at her.

Allowing a playful giggle to escape, Kate rolled her eyes. She shimmied until the pants glided down her legs to pool at her feet.

Holden stepped back to admire her smooth delicious body. Gazing at the tiny tuft of curls at the apex of her thighs, his mouth curled into an ornery half-smile. Meticulously, he lowered the zipper of his jeans.

Kate bit her lip. Anticipation coiled through her. Her voice was raspy when she asked, "Are we going to take this to the bedroom?"

"This is make-up sex, Kate. It just happens." Dropping his jeans to the floor, his erection sprung free.

Good God, this man knows how to distract me. She was powerless, and she didn't care. Kate's groin clenched with want. Pressing his arousal against her tummy, he covered her mouth with his.

She blinked back when he suddenly pulled back to grasp her chin firmly between his fingers. His eyes scorched into hers. His voice was thick with intent. "You're my only girl. Be with me. Right here. Right now."

Good God. At this point she was absolutely certain that if he wanted to take her on the front stoop of his apartment, she would surrender.

"You're my only girl." The words melted away the hostility that she'd been combating for hours. Holden was right: she was his, body and soul. Only right now, it was going to be her body. *Oh, yeah, cowboy make-up sex. Yee-haw.*

❧　❧　❧　❧

Thursday morning workouts at Westwood's private training track were coming to an end. Eric mopped his brow with a rag as he reined his old Quarter Horse, Ike, toward the gate. On those mornings, Eric and Ike sat at the far end of the training track to serve as the outriders. Drinking coffee, Eric would sit in the saddle while waiting for a rider to loose control of a horse. On cue, he would spur Ike into action and they would run the horse down to bring it under control. Kate lovingly referred to Eric and Ike as Bert and Ernie.

As much as Eric enjoyed playing outrider, he was most happy when it was over on this day. It was already eighty-five degrees and the humidity was through the roof.

Ike was feeling it too. He clomped along the sandy track with his head hung low and sweat dripping from his chest. He was looking forward to the shower with which his master always rewarded him. To be honest, Eric considered turning the hose on himself as well.

Mike and Shane leaned against the gate with their arms folded over their chests when their father approached. Eric glanced beyond his sons to see Punch riding Charlatan down the dirt path that led from the barn to the training track. Punch seemed at ease sitting on the imposing grey Thoroughbred. The sight urged a smile from the West patriarch. "Well, I never expected to see this," Eric called out to Punch.

Mike and Shane turned.

"He likes to go for trail rides. I think he'll make an okay outriding pony, too. I might give that a try next week," Punch said.

Mike couldn't bring himself to say anything. Punch was getting attached to Charlatan, and Mike didn't know exactly what to do about it. Punch was missing his old horse, Cody. Yet, the last horse Mike wanted on the farm was the equine version of Houdini, Charlatan.

Besides, they had a more important issue to discuss with him—Eugene.

Eric, Mike, and Shane were growing more uncomfortable with his presence. He was a good-natured soul, except he had a habit of telling the truth a little loose. Plus, everything he touched seemed to cause a fiasco.

Moreover, Eric wasn't convinced that Eugene had been looking for his cell phone when he found him on the bridge. Eric had been honing in on some bad juju from the big man. There was a look in his eyes that Eric couldn't quite identify. He didn't trust it. He still wondered why Eugene intended to end his life, or if he still had the same intentions.

Punch pulled Charlatan to a stop next to Ike.

Eyeing up the Thoroughbred, Ike wrinkled his nose. Deciding it was too hot to bother, he dropped his head lower to wait for that much anticipated shower.

Mike and Shane gave their father an urging expression. Eric let out a long breath.

Punch looked around at the dour expressions. "What?" he asked.

Eric scrubbed his hand across his jaw. "We were thinking that maybe Eugene—"

"I don't believe it," Punch said. "You want to fire him because of a few mishaps? He's doing a really good job at the shed. Doesn't that count for anything?"

"He's a good worker," Eric said. "No one's disputing that, Punch. But I'm not sure we can afford to keep him here. He's tends to be a bit on the clumsy side. He's not the most truthful individual that I've come across, and I found him at the bridge looking over the railing yesterday afternoon on my way home from a horsemen's meeting."

Punch's forehead creased with concern. "He wasn't gonna jump, was he?"

"He said he was looking for his cell phone. I hope he was. I'm very concerned that he's going to hurt someone during an attempt to hurt himself."

"Look, just give him another week," Punch said with a groan. "I'll keep him at the shed and nowhere else."

Mike's brows furrowed. He shook his head. "Why do you feel so obligated, Punch? I mean, you barely known the guy."

Punch leaned forward on the horn of the saddle. "I identify with him. When you're an overgrown ape like us, people look at ya differently. They tend to be afraid of you, especially if you're black, like me. Hell, they even deduct IQ points when you're our size." He let out an exasperated sigh. "He's tryin', just give him one more week, will ya? It may be more important now than ever."

Shame wagged its finger at the West men. Looking down at his dusty boots, Mike leaned on the gate. Shane shoved his hands into his pockets and gave a nearby rock a quick boot.

The man who he had taken under his wing as a boy urged a prideful smile from Eric. Saint Frances—personified. "Well," he said, "it hasn't been anything too serious, yet. A dip in the dirty horse water for Shane—"

"And my MP3 player," Shane said.

"Hey, that wasn't totally Eugene's fault," Punch put in.

Shane threw his hands up in surrender.

Eric shot Shane a look before continuing. "A pair of sore ribs for Mike, and ruined jeans for Kate."

"Not to mention an hour-long search for Tejan." Mike added

Eric pointed a warning finger at Punch. "You keep him at the shed laying blocks, where he's—I mean, *we're* safe." He added, "And keep him away from that damned bridge."

"Speaking of the blocks for the shed," Mike said, "Zoë called."

Punch tensed in the saddle.

Mike held up his hand. "Stay calm, Punch. She was calling to say that Mr. Miller has the rest of the block order ready for pick-up."

"Perfect timing," Punch said. "We'll be ready to start laying block tomorrow afternoon. You and Shane can pick that up today, while Eugene and me finish the footer."

"Well, there's a problem with that," Mike said. "Mr. Miller's forklift is broken down. So the blocks have to be loaded by hand. We're gonna need you two big apes to help out."

Ike stomped his front hoof. He was tired and sweaty and ready for his cool shower.

Shifting in the saddle, Eric said, "Get to it first thing after lunch." He reined the old Quarter horse toward the gate. "Oh, and Punch, make sure Eugene doesn't drop any blocks on anyone, please." With that, he spurred Ike forward through the gate to mosey up the winding path that led to the barn.

Punch pitched Mike and Shane a dirty look. Gathering up the reins, he smooched to Charlatan to follow Eric and Ike to the barn.

Mike grinned while dropping his chin down into his chest. When he lifted his gaze he was met by Shane's intense glare.

"Have you gotta a death wish or what?" Shane asked. "Eugene's bound to drop a freakin' block on our foot or our head or God only knows what he'll screw up."

But Mike's ornery grin never drooped. "I don't think so. I think my plan will work perfectly."

"What plan?" Shane asked.

"Where are we going later?"

"The brickyard." Shane shrugged his shoulders.

"And who will be manning the sales desk when we get there?"

"Zoë Miller. So?" Again Shane lifted his shoulder.

Mike chuckled. "And what kind of men is Zoë super attracted to?"

"Big men."

"That's right, my boy, *linebackers,*" Mike said, "I think Eugene is bigger than Punch, who seems totally uninterested in Miss Miller. Sooo... Zoë falls for old Eugene, and he goes to work for her father. We're rid of him, and maybe Zoë will give him something to live for to boot."

Shane's eyes brightened. "It could happen."

"Let's make sure that it does,"
Mike held his fist up. Shane tapped it with his. Game on.

Cindy McDonald

PART TWO

DOWN FOR THE COUNT

~ Six ~

Burke's foul mood had everyone on edge. The money from Eugene's last fight was gone, and so was Eugene. He had vanished into thin air. Jay and Chuck watched Burke chomp on his Big Mac and slurped down his soda like he was ready to explode into tiny pieces.

"How did he do it?" Burke asked. "He's a huge man, yet we can't find him anywhere. There're six hotels in Rosemount, and we've had them staked-out for the past two days. Nothing!" He slammed his sandwich onto the table.

The GPS on Eugene's Honda had indicated that he was in the area before it quit sending the signal. That had led Burke and his team to the Lanzville area—only to come up with nothing. There was no sign of the Honda or Eugene anywhere.

Warily, Chuck agreed. "How does a big man and a car disappear like that? Eugene don't strike me as no brainiac. He's a fighter. He took lots of hits to the head. But hey, he sure has pulled one over on us,"

Chuck was right, and it was rubbing Burke's ass in all the wrong directions.

The weekend was fast approaching. It was time to hit the streets aggressively. Sooner or later, Eugene Strom had to surface.

"Whatta ya want to do, Burke? We can't call it quits or our asses will be in a sling," Jay said.

Burke took a long gulp of his soda. "We're gonna split up," he said. "Jay, drop me at the south-end of town; and, Chuck, you'll take the north. Jay, park the car in the middle of town and work it. Me and Chuck will make our way toward ya."

"Sounds like a plan," Jay said.

"And what if we don't find him?" Chuck asked.

"Shut-up, Chuck," Burke ordered.

Splitting the team up, Jay dropped Burke and Chuck at their assigned sections of the city to scour for their errant fighter.

Walking along the street where he parked the SUV, Jay found Rosemount most mundane. He longed to return to Philadelphia where there was more action. He preferred the beat of the big city: the weaving in and out of traffic, the sound of horns honking, drivers cursing, and, yes, even the exhaust fumes that filled the streets. Rosemount had plenty of traffic and pedestrians, except it wasn't as big or loud as his beloved Philadelphia. He had a job to do. Until it was done, he was stuck in this one-horse-town.

The heat from the pavement hit him in the face. Sweat beaded on his forehead while he inhaled the last bit from his cigarette before tossing the butt into the gutter.

Leaning against a chain link fence, he ogled a pretty teenage girl trotting across the intersection in a very short skirt and a very tight tank top. Wishing he had the time to visit with her, he wiped his hand across his mouth.

Not today. Today, it was all about finding Eugene.

The sound of laughter beyond the chain linked fence caused him to turn. He was greeted by a red sign that read: Miller Block and Brick. The sign looked like it had been hanging on the fence since 1902. The once bright yellow words were now faded and barely legible. Looking past the sign, his eyes narrowed. Slipping his sunglasses from his nose to the top of his head, Jay pressed his face into the cold metal caging. A huge black man and two white men were loading blocks into the bed of a dark silver dually pickup truck parked in the middle of the brickyard.

What drew him in for closer inspection was beyond the truck. He could see a very large blond man talking with a woman. He grabbed the chain links with his hands. Quickly, he crept along the fence and ducked behind the blocks piled along it to get a better view of the man.

This may be the break they had been hoping for!

Zoë Miller was in heaven.

When the West boys had walked into the brickyard after lunch, not only did they bring Punch, but they had also brought along a hulk of a man named Eugene Strom. He wasn't a particularly handsome man. His face wore several scars and his eyes looked a bit haunted, but his size had her totally spellbound. He was simply huge. His shoulders were broad. His chest was wide. His muscles bulged from his shirt sleeves. His hands were rough and calloused, but they were enormous. His smile lacked confidence, yet it was gentle.

Goodness gracious. He was bigger than Punch. Zoë didn't think that was possible.

Everything that was female inside her clenched. She had it bad for Punch, but he didn't seem to want any part of her. *Perhaps a show of interest in Eugene will stimulate a response from that big galoot. Hey, it's worth a try.*

When Punch entered the sales office, she went to hook her arm through his. He favored her with that high wattage smile of his, but avoided her touch.

Mike was quick to introduce Eugene, and he made a point of telling her father about Eugene's masonry background.

Harris was most impressed, but then again, blocks and bricks had been the Miller's business for many generations. Young men who knew anything at all about masonry work was very rare these days.

Harris quickly put Punch, Mike, and Shane to work loading the blocks into Mike's truck, while Zoë cornered Eugene at the far end of the brickyard. She had managed to seat him on a short pile of bricks. Fidgeting, he attempted to peer over her shoulder to see what the boys were doing and how much progress they were making in loading the blocks.

Zoë stroked Eugene's biceps with her long finger. Her blue eyes were bright and hopeful while she interrogated him. "So where did you work before you came to Westwood?"

"Oh, here and there. My last job was bricking-up the windows for a strip club," he lied.

Zoë giggled. "I suppose they don't want people peeping into those places."

"No ma'am. They want you to pay for what you see in those kinds of clubs—that's for sure." He attempted to stand. "I should go help the boys—"

Zoë pressed him back down. "So you work as a private contractor?"

Eugene rubbed the back of his neck. "Um…You might say that."

❦ ❧ ❦ ❧

Punch wiped his sweaty forehead with his upper arm and he glanced in Zoë and Eugene's direction. His lips tightened into a thin line. "Zoë seems pretty smitten with Eugene, doesn't she?" he said to Mike and Shane while they schlepped heavy blocks to the truck.

Heat, sweat, and exhaustion tugging at him, Mike pitched Shane a mission accomplished smirk. "Sure does."

Punch's eyes narrowed. "Wonder what they're talking about."

"Zoë never lacks for conversation." Mike draped his arm over Punch's shoulder to take a gander at his stroke of genius. "Hmmm, maybe he's gonna be her date for the dance Saturday night."

"Maybe..." Punch's murmur almost revealed his tug of regret.

"What do you care anyway?" Shane asked.

"I don't," Punch insisted. "Gets her outta my hair." He returned to the task of loading the blocks onto the truck—although he found himself peeking over his shoulder at the pair more often than not.

An ear-to-ear grin beamed across Mike's face. Shaking his head, Shane chuckled. The two brothers bumped fists.

Jay couldn't believe his eyes. Eugene Strom was sitting in the brickyard talking to the dark blonde-haired woman. His lips curled in satisfaction that he had found their mark. This ridiculous gig in Rosemount would soon be coming to a close. He couldn't help but wonder what Eugene's relationship with the woman was. Did he give her the money? Was she the reason he ran to Rosemount? Had he been hiding out with her all this time?

He slid his sunglasses from his head onto his nose, and jogged through the traffic stopped at the red light to the GMC Terrain parked across the street. He would wait and watch with a pair of binoculars. At this point, he didn't want to give Eugene any inkling that he had been spotted. He slipped his cell phone from his pocket. Burke was going to be most pleased.

Finally the blocks were loaded into the bed of Mike's pickup truck.

Taking pity on their sweaty bedraggled appearance, Zoë delivered a tray with a pitcher of iced tea and glasses filled with ice. She couldn't take her eyes off Eugene, except for when she was peeking through her lashes at Punch, who managed to avoid her gaze. Her lips tipped up slightly. Punch may have been avoiding her glance, but he was more fidgety than usual. *Take that, McMinn.*

Harris tapped Eugene on the shoulder. "I know that they're good people, and they pay well, but if you get tired of working for the Wests, let me know. We could use someone around here with your knowledge of bricklaying."

Punch nudged Eugene toward the truck. "He's not going anywhere until that shed wall is finished."

"Let's not be too hasty, Punch," Mike said.

Punch shot him a dirty look.

Zoë tugged at Punch's T-shirt until he turned to face her. He swallowed hard looking into her big blue eyes and those delicious plump lips that curled around her words. "You make sure Eugene comes to Quaide's party Saturday. We'll have so much fun dancing, and I can't wait to introduce him to my friends. He's so big, and strong, and… um…blond." Oops, she had a little trouble with the last part, but she recovered quickly. She was quite certain that Punch got the idea. She saw a tiny flinch in his upper lip.

"Oh, I'm not much of a dancer, Zoë," Eugene told her.

Zoë wasn't giving up the ship. "Don't worry. Punch is a good dancer. He'll teach you. Won't you, Punch?"

Punch hesitated. His spine stiffened. "Sure," he said with the lift of a shoulder. "Well, let's go, guys. We've got lots to do."

On cue, they returned their glasses to the tray and piled into the club-cab of the truck. Eugene felt a wave of relief to break free from Zoë when the truck roared to life and rolled toward the gate that opened onto the street. Closing his eyes, he let his head drop against the headrest.

Grateful that a black SUV hesitated long enough to let him through, Mike eased the truck into traffic. The GMC fell in line behind him. *Thanks buddy.*

❧   ❧   ❧   ❧

It was a rare occasion, but sometimes Doc Spears would let Kate go home early. A gruff man, he hid his tender side, but it was alive and well. Every so often, it would shine through his steely surface. At seven o'clock, he turned to Kate and insisted that she take the rest of the evening off.

Shocked, she tried to convince him that it wasn't necessary, but Doc wouldn't take no for an answer. He all but threw her out of the vet truck.

Kate considered going to Holden's apartment to wait for him, but then decided that she hadn't seen much of her father lately. His girlfriend, Jen Fleming, had been visiting her son in Philadelphia for the past week. Even though Kate hadn't been around too much, she knew that he missed Jen. Thinking that perhaps a Friday date night with dad was just what they both needed—a little quality father/daughter time, she dialed-up Pepe's Mexican Grill to order the best fajitas in the Rosemount/ Lanzville areas.

The house was draped in quiet when she slipped through the front door. The only sound was the steady tick of the grandfather's clock in the foyer. A soft glow filtered into the foyer from the study. She peered in to find Eric in a wing-backed chair with his bifocals parked on his nose. He was reading a book while sipping a glass of wine.

Kate made a showing of clearing her throat.

Rather surprised to see her, a wide smile spread across his face at the sight of his lovely daughter standing in the doorway.

Smiling, she held up the bag of Mexican take-out that she had picked up on her way home. "Friday night fajitas with your little girl?" She shook the bag to entice him.

Setting the book aside on the end table and tossing his glasses on top of it, he said, "I can't think of anyone else I'd rather have fajitas with."

Kate laughed. "Whatta liar. You miss Jen terribly. Admit it."

The corner of his mouth lifted into a half-smile. "I do miss her. But that doesn't mean I don't love spending time with my little *snicker doodle.*" He took the last sip of his wine and deposited the glass next to his book.

Kate giggled. "I don't remember that ever being one of your pet names for me."

"Sorry... It was the best I could do in the spur of the moment."

She cast him a questioning look out of the corner of her eye. "Do you have pet names for Jen?"

He crossed the room to peer over her shoulder into the bag that was sending a waft of delicious aromas. "None that I care to share."

"Fair enough." Kate spread out the food on the coffee table. "Are you going to marry her?"

"If she asks."

Drawing in a dramatic breath, Kate said, "You're awful."

"I prefer strategic. Would you marry Holden, if he asked?"

She stopped in her tracks. *Would I? Lord knows I'm crazy about him, but something isn't right.* She couldn't figure out what it was.

"You're my only girl." It was only last night that he said those words to her before he made the most spontaneous amazing love to her in their six-month relationship—right there on the floor by the door. It was sensual, it was primal, and it took her breath away. He had dubbed it as "make-up sex." She considered being angry with him more often. Afterward, he swept her up into his arms, carried her into the bedroom, and laid her gently between the sheets, where she spent the rest of the night sleeping against him, breathing in the scent of him. Sweet replete. There was no question. She believed that indeed she was his one and only.

Yet he was so tense when she had left to go home for a shower and to change out of the pajamas that she'd shown up at his door wearing for real clothes.

What's the root of his mood swings?

She was convinced that it had to be something other than her ex-sister-in-law.

But what, or who?

Returning to her father's original question, she realized that no, she could never make a marital commitment to Holden until she knew the answer. He had to find a way to deal with whatever or whoever was causing his trepidation. With that notion, she snorted at herself. The reality was that Holden hadn't asked her to marry him. Still...

"Kate?" Eric asked.

She was jerked from her thoughts. By the look on her father's face, he'd been trying to get her attention for several moments. She blinked back. "I'm sorry. What did you say?"

"I thought we could sit on the porch. Is everything okay?"

"Oh, yes. Good idea. Let's sit outside."

Eric studied her while they gathered the bags and the napkins. Her preoccupation was unmistakable. He cocked his head to the side. "You didn't answer my question."

She turned to him with lifted brows.

Opening the front door for her, he repeated, "Would you marry Dr. Reese?"

"I'd rather eat fajitas with you ... for the time being, anyway."

Eric chuckled at his daughter's forestalling. "Fair enough."

The unrelenting humidity clung to the night air. Moths danced and dipped around the lanterns that shone down on the partially-built block wall.

Eugene straddled the structure while Punch lifted the last block of the row into place. Eugene tapped the block with a hammer, and then laid the level onto it to eyeball its placement. When he was satisfied with its position, he stepped away from the wall to stretch his back. His muscles were tired and sore. It felt good. He hadn't realized how much he actually missed working with his hands. He yawned into his fist.

Punch slapped him on the back. "I don't know about you, but I've had enough for one day. I'm headin' home. C'mon, I'll drop you at the bunkhouse."

Taking a long swig from a bottle of water, Eugene sat down on an over-turned bucket. He pursed his lips in thought. "Are you going to that dance tomorrow night?"

Punch swiped his sweaty face with a rag. "Sure. There's always lots of food at those things, and I like to dance a little. You're coming, aren't you?"

Eugene scrubbed his hand across his bristly chin. "I don't think so. I'd be like a bull in a China shop at something like that."

"I could teach ya some moves. It's not hard at all." Punch strolled to a nearby shelf where the radio was tuned to a country western station. He turned the dial until he found a solid beat. Smiling, he nodded his head and swayed while making his way to the middle of the shed. Pumping his arms and shuffling his feet, he spun in a tight circle.

Chuckling at his sure-footed friend, Eugene watched in wide-eyed wonderment. "I dunno, Punch. I don't think I can dance like that. You know what they say about white guys."

Punch laughed. "C'mon, dude. It's easy." He pulled Eugene to the middle of the shed. Considering his posture carefully, he pushed Eugene's shoulders back and straightened his torso. "That's better. Okay, now, move your feet side to side like this." Slowly, Punch demonstrated the foot movement while encouraging Eugene to join in.

His face tight with concentration, Eugene attempted to recreate the movement, but his body and his feet didn't want to cooperate.

Punch stood back to watch. He winced. "Sweet Jesus, Eugene, you're makin' Jim Parsons look like a brother."

Eugene blew out a frustrated breath. "I told you."

"Just move your feet side to side. Like this." Punch slowed his movement, and Eugene managed to follow a little better. "Relax. This ain't *Dancin' with the Stars*. It's more like dancin' with a bunch of rednecks."

Eugene chuckled at the suggestion of him dancing with the pretty blonde on *Dancing with the Stars*. He didn't know her name. He'd only seen the show a few times. He could only imagine how many bones he would break in the poor girl's body when his feet became entangled and he tumbled on top of her—on national television. *Yikes.* "I look stupid."

"So what's new?" Punch laughed. "Okay, seems like you've got the feet. Now, add some arms."

Eugene wasn't exactly sure what Punch wanted, so he pumped his arms up and down. He looked like a chimpanzee entertaining the crowd at a zoo.

Punch's eyes widened in horror. "Whoa, don't get carried away, dude. Keep them level." Punch snapped his fingers to the beat, with his arms bent at his elbows near his waist. When Eugene mimicked his movement, Punch said, "That's better."

Eugene was beginning to relax. He was starting to feel the beat, even though Punch danced more like Michael Jackson, and Eugene resembled one of *The Three Stooges*.

The music was suddenly silenced when the radio slammed to the floor. "What the hell are you doing?" Burke yelled.

Punch and Eugene snapped their attention to Burke, flanked by Jay and Chuck, filling the doorway. Their guns were drawn.

Their eyes trained on the guns, Eugene and Punch drew back a few steps.

Eugene swallowed a thick slog of saliva when Burke stepped toward him. "Took us a while to find you, Eugene, but I never thought I'd find you… like this."

Punch stepped forward. "What's this all about?"

Burke raised a hand in warning. "Take it easy, *Twinkle-Toes.* Your friend knows what I'm here for." He strolled toward Eugene with a scorching stare. His voice flattened. "Where's the money, Eugene?"

"I told you before, I don't have the money," Eugene said.

Burke spit out a cool chuckle. "Maybe your dancin' partner knows where it is. How about it? Where's he got it stashed?"

Punch's expression was impassive. His eyes locked with Burke's. Now the reality of Eugene's problems had come to the forefront. *What the hell is he mixed up in?* He knew diddly squat about Eugene's past. In the passing days, he had waited patiently for him to confide in him. It didn't happen. It was way too late for that now.

Punch stood rigid locked into Burke's cold stare.

Suddenly, Burke slugged him in the gut hard. Punch folded in half. Swiftly, he swung his leg around to kick Punch in the side to knock him to the floor with a grunt.

Unable to contain his agitation, Eugene lurched forward to slam Burke to the floor. Jay was quick to react. He dashed from the doorway to shove his gun into Eugene's temple.

If Eugene didn't know where the money was, they were dead meat. Punch had no intention of dying execution style—not without a fight. He swung his leg around to kick Jay's hand, the gun flipped from his hand and exploded.

Eugene's head jerked backward while he dropped to the floor.

~ Seven ~

T he fajita slopped down the front of his shirt when Eric jumped to his feet. Kate froze mid-bite at the sound of gunfire coming from the direction of the broodmare shed. "What the hell is going on up there?" Eric demanded to know.

"Oh, my God," Kate gasped. Slowly, she rose from her chair. "You don't think Eugene had a relapse?"

He tossed what was left of his fajita to the napkin on the table. "Stay here."

While trotting down the porch steps toward his SUV that was parked in the driveway, Eric prayed that his worst fear of Eugene attempting another suicide and hurting someone else hadn't become a reality in the broodmare shed.

He looked across the way to see Mike rushing out his door, while pulling a T-shirt over his torso. He must have heard the shot as well. Eric drove down the driveway past the barns toward Mike's bungalow.

Jay dug out from under the bales of hay that had collapsed on top of him when Punch pitched him backward. His eyes widened when he realized that he had shot Eugene—the man they had been searching for and the only link to the missing money. Now he was flat on the floor with blood spewing from his head and the big black guy hovering over him.

Burke shot Jay a look that could only mean one thing: *You're a dead man.*

Panicked, Jay searched through the scattered hay for the gun when suddenly the sound of a vehicle bumping along the dirt road outside jerked the three desperados' attention toward the door.

"Punch!" a husky voice called out from below the shed. "What the hell is going on in there?"

The sound of car doors slamming and running feet sent alarm through the shed.

Waiting for direction, Chuck's face was flushed. His gun was trained on the doorway, yet his eyes were fixed on Burke.

Their orders had been to find Eugene quietly and covertly. The last thing they wanted or needed was to draw attention to their activities.

Burke looked as though he was about to combust. His eyes darted around the shed. "Let's go!" He dashed for the door with Chuck at his heels.

Jay jumped from the hay. Hesitating at the door, he scanned the floor one more time for his gun.

"C'mon!" Burke yelled back to him. He could see the silhouette of a man pushing open a gate to let an SUV through.

Jay rushed out the door.

The SUV rolled through the gate. Burke and his team raced toward the woods. They were fairly sure they could pick their way through to where they had stashed the SUV.

"Eric!" Kneeling over Eugene, Punch pressed his hand against his head to keep pressure on the wound. "I need help right away!" Blood covered Eugene's face. His eyes fluttered open. Barely conscience, he reached for Punch's hand to use as leverage to pull himself up.

Mike appeared in the doorway. Eric was at his heels. The bloody mess in front of them caused them to pause.

"He's hurt," Punch said. "Let's get him to the house."

"Mike, call 9-1-1," Eric said.

Mike yanked his cell phone from his pocket.

"No!" Eugene held his hand up. "No ambulance and no police. I'll be okay. It's just a graze—looks worse than it really is. Please, Mr. West."

Eric crossed his arms over his chest. His chin dropped to his chest for a moment. When he looked up at Punch, he flashed him a speaking look that screamed, *What is he caught up in?*

Letting out a deep sigh of temporary surrender, Eric nodded toward the door. Punch draped one of Eugene's arms around his shoulder while Mike took up the other.

Kate had managed to clean away all of the blood to discover a mean graze across Eugene's head that extended from behind his ear almost to the center of the back of his head. It nearly matched the one on the other side of his head, which was close to healed. It would leave a nasty scar. After dabbing the wound with antiseptic that she had retrieved from her vet box, she held a cool compress against it to slow the swelling.

Eugene had a wicked headache and felt nauseous, but overall he was going to be okay.

In the study, Eric sat on the desk with his leg draped over the side. With his arms folded across his chest, he studied Eugene intently.

Mike was passing through the foyer with a cup of tea when Shane came through the front door. The grandfather clock chimed to announce the ten o'clock hour. Shane was a bit taken aback to find Mike at the main house so late. "What's goin' on?"

Mike hitched his chin toward the study. "We're about to find out. C'mon."

Shane followed his older brother into the room. He gasped at the sight of Eugene on the sofa. When Kate removed the compress from his head to make sure the bleeding had stopped and the swelling had eased, Shane winced at the sight of the ghastly wound.

Mike handed Eugene the cup of tea and four ibuprofens. Around a grimace, Eugene said, "Thanks."

"What happened?" Shane sank into the wing-back chair across from Punch.

Eric spoke up in his infamous Eric West "tone" that always signaled the time for nonsense was now over—fess up. "I think it's time you tell us what this is all about, Eugene."

"I'm sorry for all this, Mr. West," Eugene said. "I don't want to get your family involved."

"Too late," Eric replied.

"I'll leave in the morning. They'll follow me. They have been for almost six months." Eugene tossed Kate a coy smile. Gingerly, he took the compress from her hand and pushed up from the sofa. With even more care, he made his way to the stone fireplace. Waiting for the dizziness to pass, he stared at the logs that were stacked up in the fireplace while waiting for cooler weather. How comforting flames dancing among the logs would have been.

"You've gotta put an end to it, Eugene," Punch said.

Eugene let out a laugh. "Hey, that's what I was trying to do on the bridge."

"That's not the answer," Punch said. "Tell us what's going on. Maybe we can help."

Nausea swirled around him. Dropping his elbows to his knees, Eugene sank onto the hearth. With a nod of his head, he rubbed his face. "My father was a bricklayer. He had a good business, and we lived comfortably. Well, that is 'til the IRS said he hadn't paid any taxes for a while."

"Tax evasion?" Mike asked.

Tentatively, he replaced the compress to his head and winced. "Tax evasion and a healthy drinking habit. The IRS pretty much took everything. My mom left, and I was left to my own devices, you might say. I spent my late teens and early twenties working odd jobs and taking care of my dad." He glanced at the captivated expressions around the room. His head throbbing, he leaned back against the stone wall. "I was workin' as a bouncer at a dive strip club, when some guy approached me. He said that I could make a lot of money as a fighter. What the hell. I gave it a try. I ended up stayin' in the ring for fifteen rounds my first fight."

"Not bad." Punch was impressed.

"Was that before or after you worked for the governor?" Shane dryly inquired.

"Maybe it was before the circus and the white lions," Kate said.

Punch tossed them a baffled look.

Eugene looked down at his feet. "Anyway... I trained hard and I got pretty damned good at fightin'—you know, in them fight clubs. It's illegal as hell, but there's a lot of money involved. A man my size can knock another guy flat pretty quick. Anyways, I was getting a lot of fights, so I got myself a manager."

"Is that who this Burke is? Your manager?" Eric asked.

"Naw, he's just a cheap gangster whose boss talked my manager into having me throw a fight. They took in a ton of bets, but..." He shook his head. "I just don't roll that way. I tried to lose, but it was too damned easy of a fight. Shit, I knocked the guy out in the third round."

He couldn't help but notice the raised eyebrows and exchange of glances around the room. They were impressed or trying to decide if he was telling the truth.

"Burke's boss was pretty pissed," Eugene said, "so I figured I'd better lay low. Evidently, the money turned up missing. Somehow, they think I've got it. But I don't. Just let me be on my way before anything else happens."

"Who's Burke's boss?" Mike asked.

"Don't know," Eugene said with a shrug. "I'm not always told who sets up the fights. Remember, these fights are illegal. People don't like to have their names associated with them. I don't know if it's someone from around here or not. That's why I think I should go. It could be somebody who knows the layout of your farm. They know that I'm here, now."

"You're not going anywhere. No one comes onto my farm, flashing a gun and knocking people around. We'll get to the bottom of this together," Eric said.

Punch saw Eugene eyeing the door. "You can stay at my place tonight. I've got a comfortable couch."

"Seriously, I think it would be better if—"

"It's settled," Eric said. "You stay with Punch tonight, and we'll get this ironed out. Now, go ahead with Punch. It's been a tough evening."

Shaking his head, Eugene tossed his hands in surrender. Punch hitched his thumb toward the foyer. Knowing he had lost the battle, Eugene pushed to his feet, waited for the room to stop spinning, and then he followed Punch out the front door.

After listening to Punch's truck rolling along in the gravel to leave the driveway, Mike rested his elbows on his knees. "Interesting story."

Eric raked his fingers through his hair. "Yeah." He picked himself off his desk and plunked down in his leather chair behind it. "I have to wonder how much information he's leaving out." He picked up the phone.

"Who are you calling?" Kate asked.

"Lugowski," Eric said.

"But Eugene said he doesn't want the police involved," Mike reminded him.

"I'm more concerned for Punch's safety than with what Eugene wants."

The soft glow from the street lights filtered through the bedroom window. Listening to the ebb and flow of the nighttime traffic from the street below, Punch stared at the ceiling fan overhead. Sleep was elusive. His mind was too wired with Eugene's predicament. Why were these men so convinced that Eugene had the fix money? They've been following him for over six months. If Eugene didn't have the money, wouldn't they have figured that out by now? Could Eugene be lying? He had to prepare himself for the possibility that Eugene wasn't what he appeared to be.

Eugene was a desperate man standing on the edge of a bridge when Punch found him only four days ago. Dead set on suicide—wanting to end his own life, rather than continue to be chased like a wild animal. The three thugs had to be connected to a gang, or maybe even the mob. If either group suspected that you had something that belonged to them they would hunt you down until they either got what they wanted or killed you.

Eugene was in a bad situation—no doubt.

Closing his eyes, his thoughts meandered to Zoë. She was insistent that Eugene come to the barn dance at Quaide's farm tomorrow night. When they went to the brickyard, she was completely enamored by Eugene's size and bashful demeanor. She was falling all over him. It agitated him. The woman was usually flirting with him. *How can I blame her for deciding to move on? I haven't given her any hope of a relationship with me. Nonetheless, the last thing I want for Zoë is to get caught up in this hot mess with Eugene.*

A fat grey-striped tomcat jumped onto his chest to interrupt his self-doubting deliberations. With a half-smile on his lips, Punch rubbed the old cat's head. "What's up, Bart?"

Oh yeah, Bart was one of Punch's rescues. Bart was missing his left eye, and his right crippled paw curled underneath him. Punch had brought the injured cat home to live with him six years ago. Bart purred and cuddled against the chest of the man who had saved him from certain death if he'd been left to fend for himself in the barn.

Pushing up onto his elbows, Punch realized that he needed to talk to Eugene about Zoë—man-to-man. They were going to the dance, but he didn't want Eugene getting too cozy with Zoë—for her safety and her well-being.

After carefully placing Bart on the pillow next to his, Punch swung his legs over the edge of the bed and padded across the room to a stuffed chair that rested in the corner. The old cat curled into a ball to sink into the pillow. Punch yanked his jeans from the chair to quickly pull them on.

Yep, he needed to discuss Zoë's best interest with Eugene. *No time like the present.*

The moment he opened his bedroom door, he caught a glimpse of Eugene twisting the deadbolt on the front door. Punch flipped on the lights. Flinching, Eugene whirled toward him.

"Where the hell are you going, Strom?"

Eugene let his shoulders droop. He dragged in a braced breath. "I don't want to cause you anymore trouble, Punch. I'm getting outta here before someone gets hurt."

"If you run now, I'll think you've got something to hide." Punch crossed his arms over his chest. He leaned against the door frame. Narrowing his eyes and cocking his head, he asked, "Or should I be thinking that already?"

"No," Eugene said, "I told you, I don't have the freakin' money."

"Good." Punch gestured for him to have a seat on the couch.

Shaking his throbbing head, Eugene sank into the cushions and rested his elbows on his knees to plant his forehead into his fists.

Punch came straight to the point. "Tomorrow night when we go to the dance, I want you to steer clear of Zoë Miller."

Eugene's head jerked up to meet his steely gaze. "I thought Zoë was the reason that I was going to the dance in the first place."

"Not anymore, bro." Punch turned to return to his room. Hesitating, he turned back. He crossed his arms over his chest and asked, "By the way, when did you work for the governor and what's this about white lions?"

Eugene studied Punch's face. It was filled with suspicion leaning toward distrust. He ran his fingers through his blond curls. "Awe, Punch, you wouldn't understand."

"Try me."

Taking in a deep breath, Eugene said, "You've got people all around you that care for you. You know what that makes you?"

Punch shook his head.

"That makes you important," he said. "You're important to a lot of people. Me? I'm just a vagabond. There ain't nobody who cares one flyin' flip about a vagabond."

Punch's shoulders dropped. His arms fell to his sides.

"I guess I was tellin' some tall tales to make people think that I was important... somewhere along the line anyway." Eugene shrugged, "As far as the stories I told Kate and Shane, I guess I got a little carried away. Sorry."

Punch rubbed the back of his neck. He felt sorry for Eugene. With no one in his life to care about him and a bunch of thugs on his tail, it was little wonder why he wanted to end his life. "Nothing to be sorry for," he muttered. "Good night."

~ Eight ~

Charlatan nickered when Punch stroked his neck while easing a saddle pad onto his back. "I know what you're hinting at, Charlie." Punch reached into his pocket and produced a peppermint. Charlatan's ears perked and his nostrils flared at the sound of the paper wrapper crinkling in his hands.

Punch was taking the gelding for an early morning ride. He needed to do some thinking, and he did his best thinking on the back of a horse. With a crooked smile on his lips he tossed the peppermint into the air. "There ya go, buddy." Charlatan snatched it in his teeth and then hung his head low to savor the flavor.

Punch stepped out of the stall to retrieve the saddle when he came face-to-face with Sheldon. Nudging Punch's pocket with his muzzle, Sheldon nickered at him.

With an irritated expression on his face, Mike leaned against the wall with his arms folded over his chest. "Notice anything *odd?*" he asked with a dry tone.

Punch tossed Charlatan a dirty look. The gelding closed his eyes as if he'd never seen the colt before. "Nice going," Punch murmured to the old escape guru before taking Sheldon by the halter and leading him toward his stall. "At least he's showing a little initiative."

"The wrong kind!" Mike said loudly.

Punch shoved the colt into his stall and made sure the latch was plenty secure. Grabbing the saddle, he returned to Charlatan's stall.

"Where are you going?" Mike asked.

"For a long ride."

"Where's Eugene?" Unnerved by the fact that Eugene was unsupervised somewhere on the farm, Mike was unable to keep the apprehension in his tone unchecked.

"He's up at the shed working on the wall."

Mike let out a relieved breath. At least he was somewhere where he couldn't cause too much of a debacle. "When you get back, we're going to start teaching Sheldon to take a saddle. It's time he takes his initiatives in a positive direction—toward the damned racetrack for instance."

Chuckling, Punch led Charlatan from the stall. "Whatever you say, boss." With that, he shoved his left foot into the stirrup, swung his right leg over the saddle, found a comfortable position, and then reined Charlatan toward the barn door.

Mike watched the pair exit the barn. The sight urged a half-smile. Charlatan hadn't broken out of his stall since Punch had been taking him riding. Perhaps he was directing his energy in another course, and that was a good thing. Maybe Charlatan had found his calling and a home with Punch—the jury was out as to whether or not that was a good thing.

He was startled when he felt something tickle his shoulder. Turning, he came face to face with Sheldon, who was nuzzling his shirt. *Seriously?*

Indecision scraped through Eugene's gut while he plopped a block into place on the wall that he was building in the broodmare shed. Every cell in his body told him to run, except he had no means to do so. His Honda was still being repaired from his run-in with the tree along the dirt road the day that he and Punch met on the bridge. Not to mention the blazing headache. His head was sweating and the wound was burning like hellfire. There was a definite throb.

Yeah, running isn't the most viable option right now.

Once the block was securely in place, he opened the cooler for a bottle of water, and then dropped down onto a pile of blocks in the middle of the shed for a much-needed break.

A slice of sunshine gleamed through the doorway onto the hay strewn over the floor. Something under the debris glinted off the sunbeam. Cocking his head to the side, he rose to see what was hidden beneath the hay. He brushed the bristly debris aside to find a handgun. He opened the clip. It was missing only one shot.

Examining it, Eugene grinned. After glancing around to make sure no one had entered to see, he shoved the gun into his waistband and pulled his shirt over it.

The red-tailed hawk called from outside. Grabbing the binoculars, he stepped out to see what she was up to. He'd hate for Punch to miss the big event that he'd been waiting for: the moment she set her babies free to the open skies. Placing the binoculars over his eyes, he discovered that it wasn't the hawk that grabbed his attention, but rather a white SUV driving through Westwood's stone entrance.

He focused the binoculars on the SUV to see who was stopping by. The vehicle came to a stop in front of the Victorian farmhouse. A tall slender man slid from the driver's seat. He was wearing a shoulder holster and a police shield clipped to his belt. The man reached into the SUV to retrieve his suit jacket. That was when Eugene noticed the caging between the front and back seat, and the subtle emergency lighting installed on the vehicle.

It was an unmarked police cruiser.

The man shrugged into the jacket and made his way toward the house.

Caressing the gun under his shirt, Eugene ducked back into the shed.

k k k k

Eric greeted Lieutenant Carl Lugowski with a firm handshake.

A homicide detective for the Rosemount Police Department, Lugowski was no stranger to Westwood. Eric led him into the study where Lugowski took a seat on the sofa.

The detective always found this room most befitting Eric West. Like the man, it was an imposing room. The massive stone fireplace was flanked by book cases and a fifty-two inch flat screen over the mantle. The sofa faced the fireplace with deep comfy wing-back chairs arranged on either side to give the room an inviting feel. The space seemed to speak with genuine hospitality: *come, sit down, and have a brandy.* An ornate liquor cabinet with beveled doors took up the wall behind Eric's huge cherry desk with the thick braided trim. The bay window lent a grand view of the farm that was the patriarch's domain.

Lugowski had the highest regard for Eric West, a man to be respected. He had raised this farm from ruin, lost his wife, and was left to raise his children alone. He wasn't afraid to get his hands dirty in order to accomplish a goal.

Most of all, Lugowski considered Eric West to be a man of high integrity—a straight shooter.

"Can I get you a cup of coffee, Lieutenant? It's fresh," Eric offered.

"No, thank you, Mr. West," Lugowski said. "I'm more interested in why you've asked me here this morning."

In turn, Eric respected Lugowski's *let's get to the point* demeanor. "Of course," he replied. "We had a situation here last evening that I think we may need your help with—on the down-low."

Lugowski's brows furrowed.

Before Eric could continue, the sound of feet trotting down the staircase in the foyer drew their attention to the room's threshold.

Kate stepped through. "I'm on my way to the track," she said to her father. Her gaze fell upon Lugowski. Crossing the room quickly to greet him, she smiled. "Carl, I'm so glad to see you."

He stood up in time to accept the warm hug that she wrapped around him.

He hadn't seen Kate in months. As usual, she took the breath from him. Her blonde mane was left to drift over her shoulders and her gorgeous blue eyes sparkled, as always. He had seen Kate dressed to the nines in evening gowns, but hot damn, he found her undeniable in those tight jeans and that clingy tank-top she was sporting. But then again, he'd find her just as delicious if she walked in wearing a gunnysack.

Kate West was what Lugowski considered a "keeper", except she was Dr. Holden Reese's "keeper"—not his. Most likely, she never would be. He relished this instant to hold her body against his—if only for a borrowed moment.

Much to his regret, she pulled from his embrace. Gazing at him with those incredible baby blues that never failed to floor him, she asked, "How are things in Gotham, Batman?"

Lugowski's mouth lifted into a wide smile. She was a sassy little thing. He loved that about her. Regardless of the fact that her father was standing but five feet away and that he was involved with Ava, the urge to grab her and kiss that sassy mouth of hers churned inside of him. Instead, he replied, "We're doing our best, Miss West."

Kate loved his boyish grin. Every time he unknowingly displayed it, she wondered if Ava realized how sexy her man was.

She seriously doubted it. "I have every confidence, Lieutenant," she said with a wink. "I wish I could stay and visit, but I'm already running a little late. You're looking great, Carl. I'm glad I got to see you." She squeezed his hand before letting go. His hand felt suddenly cold from the absence of her electric touch. Kate favored her father with a kiss on the cheek. "I'll see you later, Dad." With that, she scooped up her backpack at the bottom of the stairs and scurried out the front door.

Slowly, Lugowski sank onto the chair to find Eric studying him intently. In a cool attempt to shake it off, he settled deeper into the cushion. Clearing his throat, he said, "I'm a homicide detective, Mr. West. I don't see any dead bodies. So what's on your mind?"

"I'm hoping to avoid a homicide, Lieutenant."

Punch stroked Sheldon's neck while Mike gently placed the western saddle on his back. Sheldon nuzzled at Punch's pocket. Obliging the colt, he pulled a peppermint out.

Charlatan nickered from his stall across the aisle when the plastic wrapper crinkled in Punch's fingers. "You've had enough candy for one day, Charlie, wouldn't want you to get fat," Punch called to him. Charlatan snorted.

It was Mike who was most relieved that Sheldon was cooperating when he began to tighten the girth ever-so-gingerly. "Are you and Eugene still going to the dance tonight?" He pulled the girth a bit tauter while keeping an eye on Sheldon's hind legs.

"Yeah, I don't see why not."

"You're not worried that those three thugs might show up?"

"That would take a lot of balls," Punch said, "don't you think?"

"Maybe. You never know what guys like that will do."

"I suppose..." Punch hadn't thought of that. "I'll keep a close eye on things."

Mike stood back to study Sheldon's reaction to the saddle. The colt swished his tail, but overall seemed quite accepting of the weight on his back and the girth strapped around him. "We'll let him stand in the stall with the saddle on for about ten minutes or so, and then we'll long-line him." He let out the breath that he'd been holding while saddling the colt. "I can finally report some progress to Ol' Man Whitmore."

The morning had dragged on, but it was finally lunchtime. Keystone Downs would be closing for some much-needed maintenance on the track for the weekend. It was a rare occasion, indeed. Everyone was excited to have a free weekend.

Kate was looking forward to an entire weekend with Holden and the dance at Dan Quaide's farm.

Dan was a burly horse trainer. He was loud, rough around the edges, and a braggart. A big one. Every year, toward the end of summer, he threw a huge barn dance. Dan would post a sign in the racetrack's business office that everyone was invited, and everyone came—even those that had little use for the host. The food was always terrific and plentiful. Beer kegs would be lined up on a hay wagon that Dan would pull into the barn. His brother-in-law's country western band provided the entertainment, and hey, they weren't too bad. All-in-all it was always a good time. When Monday morning arrived, Dan would, of course, take the opportunity to brag that he threw the event of the year in Lanzville.

Okay …Whatever.

The morning workouts had come to an end.

On her way to the cafeteria to meet Holden for lunch, Kate watched the massive exodus of jockeys, exercise riders, agents, and trainers scurrying to their vehicles to get started on that much anticipated free Saturday night. The stable hands were left behind to cool out the horses and finish the barn chores. It would only be a matter of time before the backside of Keystone Downs resembled a ghost town.

The line at the counter in the cafeteria was usually quite long at lunchtime. Not today. Kate stepped right up to order a grilled chicken salad, no French fries, for herself and a double cheeseburger, potato wedges, along with a large Mountain Dew for Holden. Waiting patiently for her order, she wondered what could be taking Holden so long.

That was when an unpleasant presence drew near.

Ava leaned against the counter next to her. "I'll have turkey on rye, lettuce and tomato, no mayo. Oh, and a bottle of water. Make sure it's cold, very cold," she told the short, dark-haired woman behind the counter, who took her order with a deadpan attitude.

Ava turned. Her piercing green eyes burned into Kate's. Her plump lips turned upward into a toxic smile.

On cue, the hair at the nape of Kate's neck stood at attention.

Ava actually seemed to enjoy the passionate feelings of abhorrence that she evoked from members of the West clan—especially Kate. Moreover, Kate hated herself for allowing Ava to see that part of her. Nonetheless, there it was bleeding all over the lunch counter for Ava to lick up like a lioness on the Serengeti feasting on a downed wildebeest.

"Ya know I was so grateful for the way Holden came to my defense when Chip Walker made that pass at me," Ava said. "Holden is such a gentleman, and he's so protective of the women in his life." Ava projected the fake sincerity in her voice that Kate loathed. It made her teeth grind and her hands to ball into tight fists.

Her eyes fixed on the shelves beyond the counter filled with boxes of candy bars and pre-packaged cupcakes, Kate tapped her fingernails on the counter. Her jaw clenched. *What's taking that cook so damned long to put together my order, and where the hell is Holden?* "You are *not* a woman in Holden's life, Ava," she hissed through her clenched teeth.

"Oh, but I am. And I'm so glad that I took this position with him. We work so well together—Holden and me."

Seething, her gaze darted from the shelves to Ava. "Why don't you shut-up? Holden wants you to go back to work for Doc Spears. In fact, I've made those very arrangements. Doc has agreed to take you back so that I can work with Holden. So consider yourself down-sized as of right now, bitch!"

The dark-haired woman behind the counter nonchalantly slid a tray with Kate's order on to the counter. "That'll be eight-fifty," she said in a flat voice.

Ava laughed. "Poor, naïve Kate. Holden would never make that deal. I have way more influence with him than you know."

Kate's upper lip wrinkled in disdain. Without so much as a glance or pause, she grabbed the cup of Mountain Dew on the tray, and threw it in Ava's face.

Falling back, Ava gasped.

The woman behind the counter sighed and proceeded to mop up the sticky liquid from the counter.

Wiping the soda from her eyes, rage blew through the top of Ava's head. *The little twat has stepped over the boundaries!* Ava's temper had surpassed the flash point. "I never thought that I would say this but, I envy you Kate. Dr. Reese is one hot piece of ass, especially in the shower. Mmmm, or was it the kitchen counter that I enjoyed so much. Kind of kinky, but hey, vanilla was never my favorite flavor anyway!"

A wicked laugh erupted from the end of the counter. Both women turned to find Chip Walker leaning against it. Practically in tears, he pounded his fists with each hiccup of laughter. "I was right!" he said with glee. "Doc is doin' you both! Damn, he's one lucky sonofabitch!"

Kate was unable to exhale the abrupt breath that she had taken in. Ava was bluffing. She had to be bluffing.

"You're my only girl." It was the other night that he held her steadfast against the door of his apartment whispering those

comforting words before he made amazing love to her. He looked her square in the eyes when he made that very declaration. She believed him. She still believed him because Ava was bluffing. Or was she? Her head was spinning. *What did she just say? Holden had sex with her in the shower … And on the kitchen counter? Oh my God!*

The sight of Chip Walker practically laughing himself into a coma made her want to wretch. His words from the other day came rushing back to haunt her once more. *"Like I said, Doc, you've got the best of both worlds: redhead by day, blonde by night."*

Oh, God! Oh, God! It was all too much. She could feel her eyes betraying her with tears. She refused to let Ava witness her melt into a murky puddle of doubt and heartache. Wanting to escape as quickly as possible, Kate pushed away from the counter and ran for the door.

"Miss! You owe me eight-fifty!" the dark-haired woman called after her.

Kate barely heard her. She darted for the exit when her eyes locked with Holden's. He stood at the door with a horrified, pallid expression.

~ Nine ~

No one had to explain to Holden what had gone down. Kate's eyes screamed betrayal of the most heart-wrenching kind. She knew of his roll in the sheets with Ava the night she had come to his door with lies about Kate's relationship with Ava's lover, Carl Lugowski.

Pouring the wine, glass after glass; Ava had purred like a kitten while weaving her tale of Kate's seduction of Lugowski only to leave her and Holden on the losing side of romance. So convincing, so manipulative was the redheaded vixen and the wine, that he had surrendered to the intoxicating lie.

He had been able to keep the affair at bay by giving Ava what she wanted: a job as his vet assistant. Now it had come around to seek irrevocable justice—the killer pain in Kate's watery eyes.

His eyes darted to Ava, who was peeking at him through her lashes with surprising remorse. He wasn't fooled. The remorse wasn't for what she had done, rather for what repercussions that it bore. There were no secrets now. He was free to fire her—to be rid of her. It would be one monkey off his back. For that, he was most relieved.

Kate marched toward the door. She hoped to hold it together until she could reach the privacy of her car.

Holden grabbed her by the arm when she attempted to pass. "Kate…"

"Don't!" She jerked her arm from his grasp, yanked the door open, and darted into the parking lot. She had only made it to her car before the tears burst from her eyes, and the weeping from her throat. Fumbling madly with her keys, she dropped them to the pavement. Cupping her hand over her mouth to stifle the sobs, she bent down to retrieve them when another pair of hands snatched them up.

"Let me drive you home, Miss West," Chip Walker said. "You're in no condition to drive."

She had no idea where he came from. She didn't see him leave the cafeteria, but there he stood before her, clutching her keys in his hand. "I'll be fine, thank you," she muttered while wiping her nose with the back of her hand. She reached for the keys.

Chip pulled them away. "I'm only trying to be nice."

"You're trying to get your ass kicked!" Holden's voice boomed from a few feet away.

Chip turned. The left side of his mouth kicked up. "C'mon Doc, you're gonna have to pick between them. The redhead seems willing to share. The blonde—not so much. I'm more than willing to take your leftovers. Quit being so damn greedy."

Grabbing Chip by his shirt, Holden slammed him hard against Kate's Mustang. "Get out of my life, Walker!"

"We'll talk on Monday, Doc," Chip said while dangling Kate's car keys in his face.

Holden blinked back. Slowly, he released his grip on Chip's shirt to snatch the keys from his hand.

Chip nodded at Kate. "Hope it all works out, angel." Straightening his shirt, he walked away.

The silence stretched between Holden and Kate until finally she reached out her hand toward him, palm up. "My keys, please," she said with a turgid tone. Her eyes were filled with anger and pain.

"No deal," he said. "I'm not going to let you go home with only Ava's version of what happened between us. Let's go to my place where we can talk calmly."

"I'm not going anywhere with you."

He dropped his gaze to the pavement. With jutted lips, he studied her through the top of his eyes. With quiet authority, he said, "Get in the car, Kate." His thumb jabbed the unlock button. He opened the door, and slid into the driver's seat.

She didn't know what to do. He was in her car. It was most apparent that he wasn't going to get out. So many feelings coiled through her: confusion, betrayal, rejection, abandonment, and the worst of all, the horrid feeling of being played the fool. Swallowing back a sob that was pushing hard to surface, she felt her heart would soon shatter. Oh yeah, she was definitely that pathetic bleeding wildebeest that Ava had sunk her sharp fangs into.

The driver's side window slid down. "C'mon, Kate. You've got to give me a chance to tell my side of the story. I'm not getting out of your car until you do. We can do this here, or in the privacy of my apartment. Make your choice, but its gonna happen."

The world was spinning. Wanting to run in the opposite direction to find a quiet hideaway to lick her wounds, she ran her fingers through her hair. She was barely holding on to what little dignity she possessed when in her peripheral vision she caught a glimpse of Ava walking toward the parking lot. Her eyes darted across the parking area to see Ava's Crossfire parked only two slots away from her Mustang.

God, could this get any worse?

"C'mon, Kate."

Holden's voice joggled her back to the moment—the moment that she didn't want to be in. She turned to find her burning blue eyes locked with his pleading brown eyes. She trotted to the passenger's door, yanked it open, slid in, and crossed her arms over her chest.

"Thank you." Holden muttered.

"You left me no choice."

Through the glass doors of the cafeteria, Ava had watched Holden's angry display with Chip. As she walked toward her car, she watched him climb into Kate's Mustang. Kate looked ripped in half, but she slid into the passenger's seat and let him drive away.

Holden had it bad for her ex-sister-in-law. For that, Ava felt a flow of regret for allowing her temper to drive her mouth. The little bitch should have kept her own temper in check, and perhaps the situation wouldn't have escalated to its present fiasco.

Not to mention that she was now back in Doc Spears' employ. That really sucked.

She noticed Chip's vehicle pulling out of the stable gate and onto the highway. Almost to the door of her Crossfire, she watched Kate's red Mustang follow the same route through the shed rows toward the security booth, and out the gate.

What was it with Chip Walker and Dr. Holden Reese? Holden's temperamental mood always went into high gear when they approached Walker's stable. Why was she not permitted to accompany him into said stable? What the hell went on in there that put him into such a tail spin? Whatever it was, it had to be illegal. Doc Spears wouldn't even vet Chip's horses.

She was still pissed-off at the way Chip had man-handled her like she was a slab of meat. Only she chose when men touched her—how they touched her—and, more importantly, *who* touched her.

Her fingers hovered over the car door handle. Chip had left the backside. Most of the stables were all but abandoned for the free weekend. She glanced down at her watch. It would be several hours until the stable hands would return for evening feeding.

Hmmm… Chip Walker could use a lesson.

The twenty-five minute drive to Holden's apartment felt more like twenty-five hours.

Kate stared out the passenger's side window. She couldn't look at him. She felt as though her soul had been ripped from her body. Over the past six months, she had allowed herself to fall in love with this man, and she actually thought that he felt the same way.

What an idiot!

For the past several weeks she feared that something was going on between Holden and Ava. He had put those fears at ease with his dynamic love-making and four simple, beautiful words: *"You're my only girl."*

Again, her eyes betrayed her. A single hot tear rolled over her lashes and down her flushed cheek. The stabbing pain of heartache coiled through her like a scalding branding iron. A sob hiccupped from her throat before she could hold it back.

She felt his eyes upon her—measuring her. At least, it was out in the open. She knew the truth—the horrible, repulsive, scathing truth. God, how she wished she could go back to the night before—when she was ignorant, when he pinned her against the door and kissed her with possessive passion—before Ava enlightened her.

'Ignorance is bliss.' Hell yeah, until it turns into a dreadful reality.

Holden spent the twenty-five minute drive toward Rosewood Commons tapping his fingers against the steering wheel and staring out the windshield while not really seeing the road.

How was he going to fix this? How was he going to make her understand what a horrible mistake he'd made? What was he supposed to say? "She means nothing to me." Oh yeah, that's the oldest line in the cheating man's bible. Kate wouldn't buy it. He wouldn't expect her to.

Nonetheless, it was a fact; Ava didn't mean anything to him—not then and certainly not now. Kate meant everything to him. He didn't want to lose her. He wanted her to be in his life—forever. Was it too late? Probably.

Her tiny sob filled him with yet more shame.

Finally, Holden steered the Mustang into his parking spot in front of his apartment. He turned off the engine and looked across the cab.

Kate hugged herself while staring at her knees. She looked like hell.

His Adam's apple bobbed, as he swallowed a thick slog of saliva. "Can we please go inside and talk about what happened?"

Kate did not lift her eyes to look at him. Her voice was thick with hurt. "Whatever you have to say will have to be said here. I'm not going into the apartment."

He dropped his head against the headrest with a sigh. Kate's eyes turned to the clock on the dashboard. "You've got five minutes, Holden."

After staring at the steering wheel for several moments, Holden shouldered the door open and slid from her vehicle. He slammed the door closed behind him.

Kate flinched. *That's it? He isn't even going to try to defend himself? Seriously? I mean that little to him?* Fighting the fierce burn, she squeezed her eyes closed to no avail. The tears oozed through.

Her door jerked opened with a whoosh. Her head snapped to the right.

Holden knelt down to look her square in the eye. He stared into her hurt gaze. His voice was steady. "What happened between Ava and me was wrong. I made a mistake. I take full responsibility for what happened. I hate myself for what I let happen, but I can't change it."

Kate looked away. He grabbed her firmly by the chin to bring her back to his intense stare. "Now here's the really important part, so pay close attention: I'm in love with you. I don't want to lose you. I will be waiting right here for you to pick me up for the dance tonight."

He wasn't offering cheap excuses. There was no *"It didn't mean anything."* Moreover, he wasn't groveling. *Damn it! Shouldn't he be groveling?* His eyes never left hers. Finally, she asked, "Why the hell should I come back?"

"Because I think you love me, too, and I'm being straight with you. I should've been straight with you long ago. I was too damned scared of losing you. I still am." Gently, he lifted her chin to force her gaze to remain locked into his intense eyes and quivering smile. "Plus, we left my truck at the racetrack. I really need a lift."

He caressed her forehead with his lips. He had no right to kiss her mouth. He had no right to expect anything from her at all. The only thing he could do was hope that she'd find enough love left inside to come back. Slowly he drew away to stand up and go to his front door.

"You might have to hitch hike," she called after him.

He turned back. "I hope not, Kate."

❧   ❧   ❧   ❧

The stable door inched open.

Ava peered through.

The long aisle way was dim. All of the lights had been turned off during the big weekend exodus. Eminem's voice wafted from the radio through the stable. Most of the stables at Keystone Downs had their radios tuned to country western stations. Not Chip Walker. His horses listened to rap. Maybe that was his secret to success—his choice in music. Somehow, Ava doubted it. The aisle was neatly swept. Bales of hay and straw were piled in an orderly fashion along the walls. The horses quietly munched on hay, as if they were just as relieved for a weekend off as well. All looked still.

She slipped through the door. Some of the horses perked their ears in mid-munch to nicker at the stranger. With measured footsteps, she made her way to the door that appeared to be Chip's office. Twisting the knob, she found it to be locked, and it wasn't a cheap lock that most stables use. This one was good and sturdy.

"What are you doing here, Ava?"

Ava whirled to fall against the door.

Doc Spears scowled at her.

Dragging in a gasp of relief, she brought her hand to her chest. "Doc... I...um, was looking for Chip."

"My ass," the old horse doctor replied.

Affronted, she demanded in a loud whisper, "What are you doing here? You're not exactly a Chip Walker fan."

He folded his arms over his chest. "I came to break into his office. Try that on for size."

His candor took her by surprise.

He smirked. "I want to see what kind of illegal shit the sonofabitch is into. What's your reason?"

"Same."

"Ahhh, that's what I always loved about you, Ava—your deep concern for what's best for Keystone Downs," he mocked with a baleful look on his face.

"Doesn't matter. His office is locked up tight."

"Step aside," he said. "I haven't met a lock that I can't pick. I used to be able to pick a lock in less than fifteen seconds. I'm a bit older now, so it may take twenty or so."

"Why were you picking locks?"

Pulling a kit from his pocket, the old man hobbled to the door. "None of your goddamned business." Within the allotted fifteen seconds, the lock clicked and the door swung open. Doc smiled.

Ava fought to conceal how impressed she was with his success.

He stepped into the room before turning to her. "Are you coming?"

She followed him in leaving a small gap open—just in case.

"I understand we'll be working together again," Doc said simply to rile her.

"I can't wait," Ava snapped back.

"I can tell," he muttered.

They both peered around the room. The barn offices at the track were usually the bare minimum. Chip's office looked like an office one would expect to see in a downtown business complex. They exchanged wordless glances filled with suspicion.

Doc went to work on the locks in the drawers of the desk. Ava kept stealing glances at the door while waiting for Chip to emerge with a Samurai sword to cut their heads off with one swift stroke. Okay, maybe that was a bit overly dramatic, but he wouldn't be happy to find them poking around in his stuff. "What are you looking for?" she asked.

"Anything. Everything," Doc said.

The middle drawer jerked open and his eyes fell upon the evidence that he was searching for. His eyes narrowed into aggravation and disappointment when he saw evidence of his worst fear. Dr. Holden Reese was involved. Shit! He wanted to grab some of the proof, yet he hadn't thought far enough ahead to bring gloves. He wasn't sure that it would be a good idea to have his fingerprints on what he'd found. He stared into the drawer. Indecision rolled through him.

"Doc, did you find something?" Ava asked while watching him stare into the drawer like a cat watching a gold fish in a bowl.

"Ahhh..." was all he could say while scrubbing his fingers over his chin. Fingerprints or not, he had to have something to show the cops in order for them to come searching, right?

"Doc?"

Before he could grab anything, the sound of tires coming to a stop and an engine slowing down outside the stable caused him to slam the drawer closed.

"Someone's here!" Ava squealed in a high-pitched whisper. Panicked, she grabbed the door while looking back to see if Doc was following her. "Where should we go?"

He hobbled after her while waving his hand toward the aisle. "Into the closest stall, quickly."

Ava dashed to the first stall at the end of the aisle and un-latched the gate.

A car door slammed outside.

She looked back. Doc was ambling along. Her hands tightened into fists. "Can't you move any faster?"

"No."

Ava pushed the big bay gelding aside to hold the gate open for Doc. After he slid through, she attempted re-latching it with shaking hands several times. After the third try, it caught. Holding her breath, she turned to him. He took her by the arm, pushed her deep into the front corner of the stall, and then pressed himself against her as deep into the corner as he could manage.

"Cozy?" Doc goaded.

"Pervert." Ava growled in a low whisper.

Doc snickered.

The Thoroughbred who occupied the stall looked at them with perked ears. He snorted at them and then laid his ears flat against his head. The stable door opened and slammed.

Chip's voice sounded irritated while he spoke on his cell phone. "That's just great! That means they know about the money. Shit, they probably know where the money is! My name is nowhere near this if they get the cops involved. You got that, asshole? Keep him covered. He's bound to be alone at some point."

They could hear him open the office door, and the door slamming behind him. His voice was muffled behind the walls, but they could hear his anger exploding at whoever he was talking to.

Moments later, Chip stepped out of his office and closed the door once more. The sound of his hand shaking the knob to make sure it was secure reverberated down the aisle.

Whirling in the stall, the Thoroughbred snorted again. He kicked the back wall.

Doc and Ava jumped. They stilled when Chip's footsteps halted in the aisle.

"What the hell's the matter with you, Herby?" Chip asked. His footsteps crunched along the floor until they came to a stop outside the stall where Doc and Ava were huddled.

The horse tossed them an agitated look and then went toward the stall door. Chip's arm reached into the stall to stroke the horse's nose. Hoping he couldn't hear the combined thumping of their hearts, Ava and Doc held their breath. His arm reached around the corner within inches of Doc to dip his fingers into the horse's bucket. "You got water and hay. You're okay. Now settle down, you'll be using that extra juice real soon." Chip walked away.

They listened intently until they heard the stable door open and close and the vehicle outside start before finally pulling away.

Ava let out the breath that she'd been holding. "That was way too close."

"He's up to no good." Doc unlatched the gate and stepped from the stall.

Ava followed. Her face was flushed. She ran her hands up and down her arms.

Doc snorted while he hobbled toward the door. "Looking forward to working with you again."

"Whatever." She marched out the stable door.

Doc did not follow her. He was glad she was gone. Glancing back at the office door, he knew that he needed at least one thing from that drawer.

His worse fears had been realized. Chip Walker was into some serious stuff. Furthermore, he had the assistance of Dr. Reese. How was he getting away with it? It didn't much matter. Latex gloves or no, Doc was going back in for that evidence. It was damning evidence for the young vet, and the end result would devastate Kate. What could he do? Dr. Reese had made his choices.

☙ ❧ ☙ ❧

Kate stretched out across her bed. She had spent the afternoon trying to occupy her thoughts with a book. It wasn't happening. Lauren Carr's mystery novel simply wasn't pulling her mind from Holden. For that matter, the characters did nothing but remind her of Holden, and the squeezing pain in her chest that he had put there. Her world had been ripped in half when Ava enlightened her to the affair that she had with Holden.

A heavy sigh escaped her when she glanced down at the page she had just read. She was pretty sure that she had read chapter twelve two times, except she couldn't really remember exactly what Mac Faraday's debacle was. She would probably need to read the chapter a third time.

Frustrated with Holden and the sweeping feeling of loss ripping through her, she tossed the book to the floor and rolled over onto her back. She lay spread eagle over the bed while trying to decide if she would return to Holden's apartment before the dance.

God help her. Everything inside told her to walk away, except her heart wanted so badly to go back.

He claimed he wanted to tell her his side of the story, and maybe he actually had one. Oh, but her head told her otherwise. Her good ol' self-conscious was giving her plenty of food for thought: *Can I forgive him? Can I ever trust him again? Can I ever lie between the sheets with him and not think of Ava?*

She loved to lie in bed and look into Holden's deep brown eyes. They were so warm, so possessive, and incredibly sexy. He mesmerized her with those eyes. Ahhh, but her self-conscious was quick to question: *Are they lying eyes?*

Covering her face with her palms, she fought back with an opposing course of rationale: Holden hadn't candy-coated what happened. He manned-up and took full responsibility for the affair. He said that he loved her and that he didn't want to lose her. She didn't want to lose him. *So where do I go from here?*

Kate was in an emotional tail-spin.

She was getting absolutely no assistance from that inner-Goddess that everyone talks about. Most likely hers was huddled in the fetal position in a dark corner while rocking back and forth—down for the count. Great.

Her head throbbed. Not so tenderly, she massaged her temples with the tips of her fingers.

There was a knock at her bedroom door. "Kate…" her father's voice called from the hallway.

Rolling over onto her side, she muttered, "Come in."

Eric peered into the room. "Are you feeling okay? Mike said you never came to the barn this afternoon."

"I'm fine. I've got a headache. I needed to lie down for a while, that's all."

Crossing the room, Eric's eyes narrowed. The mattress dipped when he eased down on the edge of the bed. He noticed the book on the floor and scooped it up. "You dropped your book."

Kate took it from him and shoved it under her pillow. "Thanks." Worried that he would see the angst in her eyes, she flipped over to her tummy.

"I thought you'd be getting ready for the dance."

"I don't know if I'm going."

Uh, oh, trouble in paradise. He asked, "Do you want to talk about it?"

"No." She lifted up onto her elbow. "How did your meeting with Carl went this morning. What did you tell him?"

Eric could see something was terribly wrong with his daughter. Her eyes were swollen from tears and the tip of her nose was pink. She wasn't going to the dance? She and Holden had been looking forward to it for weeks. Furthermore, Kate was never in the habit of lying in bed with a headache. She was the type of woman who pushed through a headache or any other discomfort to do what needed done. She was so much like her mother, yet something or someone caused her distress—enough to send her to her bed.

"Dad?"

He blinked from his thoughts. "I'm sorry. I told the lieutenant what happened at the broodmare shed. He said he'd look into it. Everything's fine, except for you. What's wrong, Kate? You can tell me."

She fell back against the pillow and draped her arm over her face.

It was true. Usually, she could talk to her father. He was a great listener. He always had such powerful insight into most any situation. Only she didn't want to poison his mind against Holden. Her father would never look at him with the same respect if he knew that Holden had betrayed her—if he knew with whom he had betrayed her. The good Lord knew that she was going to struggle with that for a long time to come.

No, she wasn't ready to poison the waters.

Taking her arm from her face, she favored him with a svelte smile. There he was, sitting at the edge of her bed like he did when she was a child sick with the flu. His brows pinched in concern, he laid his hand lightly on her ankle in a gentle show of his ever present support. He respected her decision when she finally murmured, "Not this time, Dad."

PART THREE

OVER THE LINE

~ Ten ~

Bart sat on the back of the couch with his head cocked to one side so that he could watch his master's friend pace the living room.

After stopping to listen, Eugene rushed to the couch and rummaged through the cushions to retrieve the handgun that Jay had dropped in the shed. He stuffed the gun in the waistband of his jeans in the small of his back. He raked a hand through his blond curls, only to hesitate when he realized that he was being studied.

The old tomcat's one-eyed stare seemed to penetrate through him. His tail dangled to caress the cushions—as if he were reading his thoughts.

Eugene came to a stop in the middle of the room. His two eyes locked with Bart's one. Never moving his singular gaze, Bart tucked his crippled paw into his chest and hunkered deeper into the cushions. Eugene felt the urge to shoo the cat away—for the old boy to take that creepy one-eyed stare somewhere else—when the sound of the toilet flushing and the whoosh of the bathroom door opening caused him to turn.

"Okay," Punch said while stepping out of the bathroom, "let's go."

"I really don't want to go, Punch. I think I'm gonna stay here and watch some TV."

"I promised Zoë that you'd be at the dance and you're gonna be there. Besides, I don't give out dancin' lessons to just anyone." Punch crossed to the door before turning back to Eugene. "Don't forget, you get one dance with Zoë, and that's all. I don't want her caught up in your mess. I don't want her to get hurt."

Frustration surged into Eugene's voice. "What the hell's the matter with you, McMinn? Why don't you admit you've got a thing for this woman? Hey, ya never know, she might feel the same way."

Punch grabbed the door knob. "Let's go." With a shake of his head and an irritated sigh, Eugene made his way past Punch into the hallway. "See ya later, Bart," Punch said to the cat before he closed the door.

While Punch was locking the door, a tiny voice called out, "Where're you going, Punch?"

Punch turned to Mrs. Williams peeking at them over the security chain from the apartment next door. She was a sweet old lady who kept Punch's pantry full of homemade cookies. She also liked to poke around into his private matters by trying to fix him up with her granddaughter who was ten years his junior and had piercings in places that he didn't realize could be pierced—like dead center of one's cheek.

Mrs. Williams would nag at him. *"A nice boy like you should be married with children—not living in a little apartment watching TV all night."* Mrs. Williams' heart was in the right place, but Punch simply didn't appreciate where her nose tended to be.

Punch shot her a gentle smile. "I'm going dancing."

The woman's dark eyes filled with shock. "Not with him, I hope!" she gasped.

Smiling at the old woman's suggestion, Punch dropped his gaze to the floor. For a fleeting moment, he considered going with it, but he didn't want to upset her too much. He lifted his gaze to meet hers. "This is my friend, Eugene. He needed a lift to the dance tonight."

"Oh." She drew her hand to her chest in relief. "Well, you boys have a good time. Maybe you'll meet a nice girl, Punch. I'd like to dance at your wedding, but you'd better hurry it up. I'm living on borrowed time as it is, ya know."

"Yes, ma'am," Punch said.

The old woman eased the door shut.

Eugene turned to him. "You've got people worrying about you everywhere, don't you?"

"So it seems," Punch said.

Dropping his head against the headrest, Burke took a long drag from his cigarette. Watching the big black guy's apartment building, they had been parked along the street for several hours. They were stuck in the heat and without any shade. A blue haze lingered in the vehicle from the dozens of cigarettes that had been inhaled during the course of the torturous surveillance. The radio stations changed from rap to rock to rap to pop and to country western.

Sweat dripped down Burke's temples. He turned toward the passenger's seat where Jay poked at the buttons in search of yet another suitable music station. His eyebrows furrowed into a "V" while he searched the airwaves. Blowing smoke from his nostrils, Burke fidgeted for a more comfortable position.

From the back seat, Chuck lurched forward to smack Burke on the shoulder. "They're comin' out." He pointed through the windshield to across the street. Burke and Jay jerked to attention.

Punch and Eugene strolled out of the apartment building and climbed into Punch's red Dodge Ram pickup parked in the lot next door.

Burke started his truck and shoved it into *DRIVE*. "'Bout damned time. What the hell is Eugene doin' with this guy? Playin' house?"

Jay laughed like a hyena.

Shooting him a glare, Burke pulled the vehicle into the street several cars behind Punch's truck.

Holden paced back and forth across the front of his apartment building. If Kate didn't soon show up there would surely be a deep rut. He glanced up the street again—empty.

He looked down at his watch. She was fifteen minutes late. He eased down onto the steps that led to his front door, dropped his elbows onto his knees, and his chin into his hands.

What the hell did he expect?

Okay, she had taken a shower, a very long hot shower. Kate curled her blonde locks into a cascade of loose curls that swept across her shoulders. She slipped into the soft blue sleeveless peasant blouse that Holden loved so much. Just as quickly she whipped it off and tossed it onto her bed. Why on earth should she wear his favorite shirt? The bastard cheated on her—with Ava no less! Wear his favorite shirt?

Ludicrous!

For that matter driving to his apartment complex and parking right inside the entrance was simply insane, except that's exactly where she was—sitting inside her car with her head upon the headrest, biting on her lip, and trying to breathe while deciding whether she was actually going to venture two streets over to his apartment.

Indecision rolled through her. Her gut clenched as her hand clumsily grappled for the gear shift. This was it.

What's it gonna be, West?

❧ ❧ ❧ ❧

Holden's backside was getting stiff. Checking his watch again, she was now twenty-five minutes late. Heat lightning sliced through the purple drape of dusk. A long submissive sigh escaped from deep in his chest while he pushed to his feet.

A crack of thunder accompanied a burst of lightning. Maybe they would get some much needed rain. Holden took one last look up and down the block. A silver Optima rolled around the corner and then turned into an apartment across the street. Pulling his keys from his hip pocket, he stomped up the steps to let himself into his apartment. His heart felt like a boulder inside his chest. Kate wasn't going to show up on his doorstep in pajamas—not this time. The one thing that was right in his screwed-up world was as good as gone.

He closed the door, slammed the keys onto the kitchen counter, and pulled his shirt out of his jeans to allow it to fall loose around his waist.

Grabbing the remote, he flopped onto the couch. He yanked his cell phone from his pocket in hopes that he'd missed a text. Nope. He thumbed the button for his contacts while considering one last plea for her forgiveness.

The sound of a horn honking summoned him from his seat. He made haste to the window and pinched back the curtains that Kate had made him buy. There she was in his parking spot. She was honking the horn.

He dashed out the door and down the steps. "Hey, I was getting worried."

Kate dragged her gaze to his. "Get in. I don't know where we go from here, Holden, but we need to talk."

"Do you want to come inside?"

She didn't trust herself. She couldn't absolutely, without a doubt, trust that she wouldn't allow him to apologize in his oh-so-sexy-Holden way. She couldn't trust that she wouldn't succumb to his sensual, amazing "make-up sex." *If I let that happen, then where will I be?* "Absolutely not," she told him.

He wasn't going to argue with her. She'd shown up to talk. Praying that it was a good sign, he jogged to the passenger's side of the car and slid in.

Hey, it was better than nothing.

∽ ∂ ∽ ೪

Punch eased his pickup off of the gravel road and through the ruts and bumps of the field at Dan Quaide's farm that was used for party guest parking every year.

In the short distance, he and Eugene could see the barn was lit up festively. A crowd moved about inside the barn loft.

Usually the loft was filled with tractors, hay wagons, and a hay baler. Dan had moved all the farm equipment out to make room for the big to-do. While they searched the field for a place to park, the sound of random drum beats and guitar cords wafted through the open truck windows. The band was warming up.

Punch waved to a group of girls who were making their way from their vehicles toward the barn. Waving their arms at him, they hooted while jumping up and down. Laughing, he shook his head at their silly antics.

While driving through the sea of vehicles, Punch noticed some familiar ones: Mike's silver dually pickup, Eric's black Denali, and even ol' Doc Spears' vet truck. He pressed the brake to pause a moment to let Lugowski and Ava pass hand-in-hand in front of his truck.

Lugowski nodded at him. Punch nodded back.

Eugene was focused on the crowd at the barn. He couldn't believe how many people were there. "You didn't tell me that the party was gonna be this big."

"Oh yeah, Dan Quaide puts on quite a shindig every year." Punch looked across the cab to see the trepidation that filled Eugene's posture and expression. "Don't be such a stick-in-the-mud, Strom. It'll be fun."

Eugene looked out over the dark field lined with cars and pick-up trucks, and again to the crowd pouring into the barn. "I dunno, Punch."

Finally, locating a parking spot toward the edge of the field, they climbed out of the truck. They made their way through the bristly grass to the barn. Laughter, conversation, and the annoying thump of a microphone being prepped filled the night.

The old bank barn butted up against the field and then the ground fell away over an embankment to the stabling area where Dan housed about fifteen Thoroughbreds.

A wide thick ramp led into the loft where the party was well underway. The ramp always reminded Punch of a bridge over a moat. It gave and creaked under their feet when they crossed.

Brightly-colored party lanterns of blue, yellow, orange, and pink strung across the open beams greeted them. The band was set up in the far corner on a platform made of two-by-eight boards. Dan had pulled a hay wagon along the back wall to accommodate many kegs of beer, and an enormous banquet of food. Bales of straw lined the perimeter of the loft for seating.

Zoë filled a red solo cup with a frothy beer and was handing it to Mike when he looked up to see Punch and Eugene in the barn's doorway. He grinned from ear to ear, while gently nudging Zoë's attention in their direction. Zoë's eyes brightened. Quickly, she ran her long fingers through her hair to fluff it. She tossed a wink in Mike's direction, and then nimbly made her way through the crowd to greet them.

Zoë slipped her arm through Eugene's, which made him flinch in surprise. "High time you two showed up."

Punch opened his mouth to speak. Seeing his attempt out of the corner of her eye, Zoë put her plan of making him jealous into play by whisking Eugene away. "C'mon, Eugene, I'll introduce you around before the dancing begins." Zoë dragged him toward a group of young women. She felt a little bad about ignoring Punch, but if it got his attention then it would be worth it in the end.

Eugene glanced helplessly over his shoulder at Punch, who pitched him a warning look.

Punch felt a hand clap onto his shoulder. "Told ya to latch onto her," Mike said into his ear. "Now it looks like you're a day late and a dollar short, dude."

Punch's jaw tightened.

∽ ∾ ∽ ∾

Burke managed to wedge the Terrain into a space between two pickups with a fair view of the barn. It was a tight fit, but they were strategically placed. Chuck leaned forward with his elbows resting on the front seats.

Through the windshield, they watched Punch and Eugene go into the barn. Burke locked eyes on Chuck in the rearview mirror.

Shrugging, Chuck asked, "Now what?"

"We wait." Burke said.

"Wait for what?" Chuck asked. "There's too many people, man. No way we're gettin' him outta here unnoticed."

Burke explained. "You don't know Eugene too good. He hates crowds unless he's fightin' for 'em. He'll be lookin' to grab some fresh air real quick." He reached across Jay to open the glove box to retrieve his handgun. He checked the magazine.

Chuck readied his weapon, too.

~ Eleven ~

"Let's get this party started!" At the edge of the platform acting as a stage for the band, Dan Quaide held a beer up over his head. "I wanna big round of applause for my brother-in-law, Butchie, and his band, Western Rogues!"

The barn filled with rousing applause, some whistles, and plenty of hoots.

Butchie grabbed the beer from Dan's hand to chug it down. Letting out a satisfied grunt, he said, "Get out of the way, Dan! You're holding back all the fun!"

Laughing, Dan jumped from the platform.

Without pause, the band began to play. The loft floor filled up quickly with couples dancing a two-step.

Watching the couples frolic and dance, Eric and Mike leaned against the hay wagon. "I'm surprised that Kate and Holden aren't here yet." Mike took a swig of his beer while scanning the room for his sister and her beau.

"I'm not sure they're coming." Eric said.

Mike shot him a questioning look. Before he got the chance to ask for more information, Lugowski stepped up to the keg.

"Where's Mr. Strom?" Lugowski picked up a red cup from the stack.

Eric spotted Eugene locked in Zoë Miller's clutches while talking to a group of women. Flushed, Eugene looked uneasy and in bad need of a beer. Eric hitched his chin in Eugene's direction. "He's the big blond guy over there with Zoë Miller."

After measuring up Eugene, Lugowski turned back to Eric and Mike. "And you're sure that you didn't get a look at the guys who assaulted him in your barn?"

"Unfortunately, no," Eric said.

Lugowski filled his cup with beer. "I want to talk with McMinn."

Mike nodded in the general direction of where Punch was leaning against the wall. "Have at it. He's right over there. I thought you cops weren't allowed to drink while on duty."

"I'm off duty. I just want to make sure we don't have any issues this evening."

❦　❦　❦　❦

Punch was watching every move that Eugene and Zoë made. In case Eugene's friends were to show up, he wasn't going to let them out of his sight. He was going to make sure Zoë didn't get caught in any crossfire. Her arm was still wrapped around Eugene's. She was down-right giddy while introducing him to her girlfriends.

Punch fought to suppress the gurgle of jealousy in his gut.

The woman looked so sexy in that lavender sundress with the thin spaghetti straps that barely caressed her downy shoulders.

What the hell? Eugene had even less to offer Zoë Miller than he did. Eugene was a fighter. When he wasn't doing his fight-club thing, he was nothing more than a bouncer in strip clubs. There was no question about it. Eugene's was not the type of man that Zoë should be with. *What's that girl thinking?*

Then again, Zoë had no knowledge of Eugene's past. Punch was pretty dang sure that Eugene wasn't going to be very forthcoming about it. She had to be totally enamored by his size because Eugene Strom wasn't exactly Tom Cruise.

Scrubbing his fingers across his chin, Punch was unable to take his eyes off her hair as it swept across her shoulders when she moved, the way her plump lips curled when she smiled, and the way those beautiful eyes sparkled—at Eugene.

When were Zoë and Eugene going to head for the dance floor? Because the minute that dance was over, he was dragging Eugene out of the party before anything bad could happen. Zoë would be irritated, but Punch was going to be absolutely sure that she was out of harm's way. Or was it that he wanted Zoë away from Eugene? It was the same thing, right?

"McMinn..." Lugowski's voice pulled Punch from his funk. Startled, he looked over at the lieutenant, who was holding out a cup to him. "Have a beer with me. I've got a few questions about your friend, Eugene Strom."

⋐ ⋑ ⋐ ⋑

Taysa Quaide was out of breath when Mike twirled her off the dance floor toward the keg where Eric was keeping an eye on Lugowski while he questioned Punch. The crowd clapped during the momentary pause in the music before the band played another lively tune.

Bringing her hand to her chest, Taysa gasped for air. "I don't know about you, Mike, but I could use a beer."

Mike grabbed two cups from the stack and began pouring. "I'm way ahead of you, Taysa." The beer had a rich froth when he brought the cup upright to hand to Dan Quaide's lovely daughter.

She turned to Eric. "Are you having a good time, Mr. West?"

"Yes, I am, Taysa. Your father puts on a great party."

"Where's Jen?" the brunette asked.

"She's in Philadelphia visiting her son," Eric said.

"Perfect!" Taysa grabbed Eric's hand. "I have you all to myself. C'mon, let's dance."

"I thought you were dancing with Mike," Eric said when she pulled him toward the dance floor.

"He looks tired. Besides, I need a fresh pair of feet to step on."

Raising his cup up in a toast, Mike laughed. With a shrug, Eric took her into his arms and they joined the crowd on the dance floor.

With his cup of beer in his hand, Mike drifted toward the food at the other end of the wagon. He had started assembling a sandwich when he felt a tap on his shoulder. He turned to find Jen Fleming's smiling face.

"Where's your father?"

Mike hesitated. His eyes darted to the dance floor where Eric was whirling around with Taysa Quaide who was not only a real looker but a good twenty years his junior. Yikes. Mike bit his lip. *What's she doing here?* Eric's girlfriend, Jen, wasn't expected home for three or four more days. He swallowed hard. "He's dancing with Taysa Quaide," Mike said as casually as possible while nodding toward the dance floor.

Jen's eyes followed Mike's gesture to see Eric with the pretty younger woman laughing and dancing in his arms.

"Yes, I see that." Jen grabbed him by the arm. "C'mon."

Mike abandoned his sandwich to twirl Jen onto the dance floor. Jen's slim figure complimented the red smocked strapless sundress she was wearing. Mike couldn't help but think what an attractive woman his father was involved with as they danced through the crowd until they reached Eric and Taysa.

With a wink and a smirk, Mike gave Jen a good hard whirl until she bumped into his father.

Taysa's face filled with apprehension. Mike swiftly rescued Taysa to take her into his arms and sweep her across the floor.

"Eric West, I go out of town for a week and I find you in the arms of a younger woman," Jen said as if she were affronted.

Eric's smile was wide. He swallowed her into his arms. "That will teach you to leave me unsupervised, Ms. Fleming." He pressed his lips to hers while squeezing her tightly in his embrace. "God, I missed you, woman," he whispered into her ear.

Jen's smile stretched up to her fairy green eyes.

⇛ ⇝ ⇛ ⇝

"What kind of questions?" Reluctantly, Punch turned away from Zoë and Eugene to give Lugowski his full attention

"Mr. West tells me that Eugene Strom was assaulted by several men at the farm the other night. What's the problem?" Lugowski asked.

Not sure how much intel he wanted to divulge, Punch calculated Lugowski for a moment. Eugene had made it clear that he didn't want the police involved. For some reason the guy thought that it would only make matters worse. Impassively, he said, "It was a misunderstanding."

"Over what?"

"They thought Eugene had some money, but he didn't."

"Why did they think Mr. Strom had the money?"

"I don't know, and Eugene doesn't know either."

"Where did the money come from that they thought he had? A drug deal? A robbery? Gambling debt?" Lugowski leaned against the wall with one hand in the pocket of his jeans, while the other lifted his beer to his lips.

"I just got done tellin' you that I don't know the answers to your questions," Punch said succinctly. "So if you're done having a beer with me, I'm gonna check out the food table."

No charges had been pressed, no police report filed; so therefore Lugowski had no real authority over the situation. The detective lacked his dress slacks and jacket, yet Punch had no doubt that Lugowski had his shiny badge tucked away some-where on his person.

Pushing off the wall that he was leaning against, Punch tow-ered over the lieutenant—not only in height but in bulk as well.

Lugowski wasn't intimidated. His gaze never wavered from Punch's.

"Carl, are you spending the evening with me or with McMinn?" Ava's voice broke up the stare-down.

The corners of Lugowski's mouth kicked up at the beautiful redhead. "He's not my type, babe."

❖   ❖   ❖   ❖

Eugene was never comfortable when surrounded by women. When he worked as a bouncer at the strip club, he was never permitted to socialize with the dancers. The only contact he had with the girls was when a customer got a little too friendly, and had to be redirected.

Eugene was a big galoot. Most women didn't consider him handsome or desirable—except the hard ones who at-tended his fights in the old abandoned warehouses or back al-leys. Oh yeah, those women were turned on by the brawl—by the power he had in his big fists and his ability to knock another man unconscious to the ground. Finding that exciting and enticing, they would approach him after the fight to seduce him. Hey, he was human. He was a man with needs. So he spent a little time with those kinds of women.

Zoë Miller wasn't that kind of woman. She was charming and intelligent. She had class, and he couldn't figure out why she would spend five minutes of her time with him—Eugene Strom—the backstreet fighter. He was quite sure that she was unaware of his violent occupation. However, he was aware that he had a rough look about him.

Nonetheless, there he was with Zoë Miller's arms looped through his—standing smack-dab in the middle of her girlfriends while they measured him, questioned him, and yes, even flirted shamelessly with him.

He hadn't bargained for this.

The women's chatter buzzed all around him, except he wasn't really hearing a word they had to say. He was too busy scanning the crowd. Burke and the boys had to be watching him. They had to show up sooner or later. Searching the throng of partiers, he noticed Punch leaning against the far wall talking to a tall thin man.

Eugene's eyes narrowed. From his distance, and with people walking through his line of vision, he couldn't see very well, but the man resembled the one who had come to Westwood. Eugene's apprehension was on red-alert. Stealthily, his hand made its way to the small of his back where he had slipped the handgun that he found into the waistband of his jeans. He was feeling the pinch of watchful eyes, not only from those who had been hunting him, but also from the nameless police officer.

As he gauged them, Eugene could see that Punch was disconcerted with their exchange. Not good. "Zoë, who is that man talking with Punch?"

Zoë glanced over her shoulder. She didn't have to search the mass for Punch. She seemed to be much attuned to his location. "That's Lieutenant Carl Lugowski. He's a homicide cop or something like that. Anyway, he dates Mike West's ex-wife, Ava." Cocking her head, she furrowed her brows. "I wonder what he's talking to Punch about. It's not like they're friends or anything that I know of." She giggled. "Maybe Punch is a suspect in one of the lieutenant's murder cases."

Eugene forced a likewise chuckle. "Boy, it's hot in here. I sure could use some fresh air. Think I'll step outside for a few minutes." He nodded to her friends, who were still eyeing him up and down.

"Excuse me, ladies." He slipped away from Zoë's grip and picked his way through the crowd toward the door.

❧ ❧ ❧ ❧

Punch was pissed. Eric had ratted on Eugene. He thought they were in agreement—no police. He chugged down the last of the beer in his cup, picked up a plastic plate, and began slapping together a sandwich.

The Wests were his family. Family didn't rat on each other. Family didn't promise one thing, and then do another. *What the hell's up with Eric? He never betrays a trust. He never lies.* The flush of agitation started at the base of his neck to make its way up to the top of his head. Suddenly, a hand clapped onto his shoulder.

"I haven't seen you on the dance floor all night. What gives?" Mike reached around him to snatch a cube of Colby Jack cheese.

Punch's irritation had reached crescendo. He felt betrayed by the people he trusted—the people he called "family." He whirled around and grabbed Mike by the shoulders to pin him into a corner.

Mike's expression was not of fear, but rather of total bafflement.

Punch glanced around. The quick movement had caught several people's attention. They were watching with furrowed brows. He kept his voice low but concise. "What the hell is going on? Why did Eric call the police?"

Undaunted by Punch's size or his mood, Mike matched his low tone. "Whoa, reel it in a bit, big guy. Dad's only trying to cover your ass. Essentially, he didn't call the police. He called Lugowski, because when thugs start showing up waving guns in people's face, it's never a simple misunderstanding. I'm guessing Dad doesn't trust Eugene's intentions, but he does care about your well-being. Why don't you calm down?"

Slowly, Punch let go of Mike's shirt. "Why didn't Eric discuss this with me?"

"Because you're too close to the situation," Mike said. "You weren't looking at things as rationally as someone who wasn't as involved. You're always busy saving the world, Punch. Sometimes you need a little saving yourself—mostly from yourself." While straightening his shirt, Mike nodded at the spectators to let them know that everything was fine.

"I don't think Eugene has the money."

"I don't think so either," Mike said. "But that doesn't mean that he doesn't know about the money. C'mon, Punch, thugs don't chase anybody for six months without a damned good reason." He hesitated for a moment while searching for the right words. He looked Punch square in the eye. "I know you want to see the good in everyone and that's a great quality. It's what makes you a great man, but I think Eugene knows more than he's letting on. Deep down, I think that you believe the same thing."

Blowing out a breath, Punch returned to his plate, picked up his sandwich, and took a bite.

Relieved, Mike hoped Punch understood where he was coming from, or at least where Eric was coming from—concern for a beloved member of their family. He glanced at Punch's sandwich. "Hey that looks good. I'm starving. Think I'll make a sandwich myself before Taysa comes looking for another dance." Mike took up a plate and grabbed a roll. He looked around the barn, "By-the-way, where's Eugene? I haven't seen him on the dance floor, either. I thought you taught him some of your *sweet moves,"* Mike goaded.

Punch's head jerked up.

Mike could see the wash of panic in his expression. "Maybe we should go look for him,"

Punch raised his hand. "Naw, I'll go. He probably stepped outside for some fresh air." At least that's what he was hoping while searching the crowd inside the barn. Where was Eugene? More importantly, where was Zoë?

~ Twelve ~

I mpatient, Burke shifted in his seat.

Jay fumbled with the stations on the radio. He found a rap station, and then a hard rock station, he soon returned to the rap, but then he switched to heavy metal.

Burke glanced to the backseat where Chuck was reclined with ear buds listening to his Ipod.

Stuck in the SUV all day, they had been sweating their asses off while waiting for the opportunity to nab Eugene. No luck.

Now, they were sitting in the middle of a hay field watching a bunch of rednecks party in an old barn. He had no idea that people still did that sort of thing.

Hillbillies.

He pressed his fingers against the back of his neck and rotated them in a circle in an effort to relieve the stiffness.

Jay decided to switch the station once more to rap.

"Pick a freakin' station!" Burke ordered.

Jay jerked his fingers from the buttons and settled back into his seat. He decided to be satisfied with his latest choice.

Burke rubbed his weary eyes with the palms of his hands. He opened them and blinked hard to refocus. Then, he spotted the movement he'd been waiting for: Eugene stepping out of the barn alone.

The need to get as far away from the party and from Lanzville as quickly as possible skittered up and down Eugene's spine. Nodding politely at strangers, he stepped onto the creaky ramp and looked out into the dark field filled with vehicles.

Lightning streaked across the sky and a burst of thunder cracked.

The small group of people smoking cigarettes outside looked up to the sky while making conversation about the hope for some much needed rain.

Trying to appear as casual as possible, Eugene shoved his hands into the pockets of his jeans. Surely, one of Mr. Quaide's guests had left their keys in the ignition of their ride. He strode down the ramp in search of old pickup trucks, beat-up, rusted out late model cars—those where the kind of people who left the keys dangling in the ignition or tossed carelessly into a cup holder. If not, he would have to hot wire one of the vehicles. He didn't care what the car looked like; it only had to get him where he needed to go.

Eugene was about to step off the ramp when Zoë called out to him, "Eugene! Where are you going? We haven't danced yet." He turned to see her hurrying down the ramp toward him. He let out a deep sigh. The last thing he needed was Zoë tagging along behind him. Or did he? With a half-smile on his lips, he said, "I'm just not very good in big crowds, Zoë. I'm sorry."

"You're gonna leave without giving me my promised dance, or saying goodbye?"

Looking into her big blue eyes, Eugene could see why Punch was so attracted to this lovely woman. He couldn't figure why he was giving her the brush-off. Was it a race thing? Punch hardly seemed like the kind of man who wouldn't accept someone because they were a different color. He was a too compassionate and giving being. It had to be something else. Whatever it was, it certainly wasn't obvious to him.

"Well, I really can't leave because Punch brought me. I thought I'd take a walk. Want to join me?" He reached his hand out to her.

Zoë hesitated. She looked at the hand inviting her and wished it belonged to someone else. Someone who wasn't taking the jealousy bait that she thought she'd dangled so cunningly. She really thought that she would stir the feelings that she thought Punch was hiding by coming on to Eugene. Obviously, she thought wrong. Punch just wasn't that into her.

She glanced over her shoulder toward the barn. Disappointment stabbed her through and through. With a sigh, she turned back to the outstretched hand waiting for her to clasp.

Eugene seemed harmless enough.

He smiled again. "I won't bite. I promise."

She bit her lip and surrendered her hand to his. They strolled along to wander deeper among the sea of parked vehicles. The low cut hay prickled his jeans and Zoë's bare ankles. The thunder rumbled and the breeze that had kicked up grabbed the skirt of her lavender sundress to make it flutter around her thighs.

"Where are we walking to?" she wanted to know.

"Do you have a car here?" Eugene asked.

Zoë planted her feet into the ground. Startled, her lips parted.

"No, no, don't get the wrong idea," he snorted. "I was thinking a drive might be nice. I really haven't seen that much of Lanzville. It looks like we might get wet if we walk too far, anyway." He lifted his face into the breeze.

Letting out the breath she'd just sucked in, Zoë said, "Mine's the white Outlander over there." She pointed to the SUV parked several vehicles down.

"A crossover...nice," Eugene said.

"Thirty-one miles to the gallon."

"That's important these days."

"I know." She asked, "Would you like to drive?"

"Sure."

Zoë dug into the hidden pocket of her dress. The breeze whipped her hair over her face.

"Yeah, what the hell's wrong with Punch McMinn?" Eugene thought.

Producing the keys, she handed them to him. He fumbled in the dark to find the right button to push.

"Ahhh, shit. Our timing couldn't be worse, boys."

Eugene whirled around to find Burke sneering at him, while Chuck pointed the business end of a forty-five at them. Burke announced, "Ol' Eugene was just about to score."

Zoë gasped at the sight of the gun-toting hooligans.

Burke raised his finger to his lips to hush her. "Shhh, we don't wanna attract any attention, honey. We only wanna talk to Eugene."

"I told you, I ain't got the goddamned money," Eugene said.

"I'm so freakin' tired of that lame answer, Eugene."

"It's the only one I've got, Burke."

"Yeah, we'll see... We'll see," Burke hissed.

Chuck raised the gun, when out of the darkness a hulk of a man dove on top of Burke to drive him to the ground.

Eugene took advantage of the shock value that his friend, Punch had provided to smack the gun from Chuck's hand into the weeds. The backstreet fighter that he kept carefully suppressed emerged when Eugene punched Chuck in the jaw to send him into the side of Zoë's Outlander. Chuck's head bounced against the vehicle, his eyes rolled to the back of his head and his body slid down the driver's side door like a rag doll.

But Jay was ready. He managed a quick right jab to Eugene's cheek. His head bobbed back but he quickly recovered and came up smiling. Dancing from foot to foot, Eugene ducked and jabbed as he'd been taught to do in the fight clubs until Jay lay on the ground in a heap of unconsciousness.

Eugene turned to witness Punch tossing Burke over the hood of Zoë's SUV with a grunt, a thump and a thud onto the ground. The two massive men exchanged glances, and then peered over the hood to find Burke lying still on the ground.

Grinning, they bumped fists.

Zoë crept from the corner of the SUV where she'd recoiled from the fist-a-cuffs. Her voice was filled with trepidation when she asked, "Are you two all right?"

Wiping the sweat from their faces and rubbing their sore fists, the two large men nodded.

Punch made his way quickly to Zoë. "Are you okay?" He caressed her cheek with the pad of his thumb. He would have died before he let anyone hurt Zoë, and he was thankful that he'd gone looking for them when he did. He hated to think what those thugs were capable of.

Zoë's eyes met his. With a shy smile, she nodded to assure him that she was okay.

Punch swallowed hard, and then turned to Eugene. "Lieutenant Lugowski of the Rosemount Police is at the party. You keep an eye on these bastards, and I'll go get him,"

Eugene tensed.

Punch slapped him on the shoulder. "Hey it's over now, buddy. Lugowski's a pretty fair guy. Tell him what happened. You don't have to run anymore, Eugene."

A half-smile crept across Eugene's lips. "Yeah... You're right."

Punch nodded. "I'll be right back."

Zoë grabbed his hand when he turned to leave. He tossed her a speaking look that left no question in her mind that he wanted her to go with him, but before he took his first step toward the barn, Eugene whipped out the gun that was hidden in his waist band and smacked Punch hard in the back of the head.

Punch lurched forward to fall onto his hands and knees. Letting out a loud gasp, Zoë stepped back in horror. Quickly, she reached for Punch who struggled to maintain consciousness while blood dripped from his head.

The world spun around him. Nausea coiled into his throat.

Zoë spun on her heels to shove Eugene as hard as she could. "What are you doing?!"

Eugene grabbed her by the arm and shoved her toward her SUV. "Sorry, Zoë, but we've got to blow this party right now."

She struggled against him to no avail.

He jostled her into the vehicle and jumped into the driver's seat. He shoved the key into the ignition. He hesitated for a moment to watch Punch still on his knees, feeling the ground while trying not to collapse into the weeds.

"What's wrong with you?!" Zoë screamed at him when he pulled away with the tires spinning and spitting clumps of dirt and hay seed into the air.

The SUV bumped and rocked through the rutted hay field. Zoë punched at Eugene, who lifted his shoulder for his defense.

"I don't wanna hurt you, Zoë! But you gotta settle down!" He struggled to steer the vehicle onto the gravel road while dodging her fists. He drove into the darkness that was split by lightning.

Finally, when he arrived at a crossroads, he rolled the SUV to a stop. He grabbed Zoë by the arm and squeezed it until the pain brought her to submission. He shook her only once to get her undivided attention. Her hair was in a wild tangle, her breaths were hitched in anxiety, and her face was flushed and sweaty.

"Listen to me, Zoë!" He shook her again until her watery eyes focused on his determined gaze through the strands of hair dangling in her face. "Listen! I didn't want to have to take you with me, but I need some insurance now that there's a cop around." He looked into the darkness that surrounded them. "Are you afraid of heights?"

Her brows furrowed and her eyes narrowed at the odd question. Shaking her again, he pressed his fingers harder into her flesh. She winced.

He repeated his question. "Are you afraid of heights?"

Her arm felt that it would soon snap under his force. She muttered, "No."

He let go of her arm and caressed it. "Good girl. Now, go in the glove box and get me your flashlight."

She looked at him as though someone had told him her secrets.

"C'mon, I know you've got one," he said. "All single women have a flashlight in their glove box. It's as standard as lipstick in your purse."

Zoë jerked her arm away and rubbed it. He had squeezed so hard that the skin looked like his fingers still gripped her.

Feeling the pinch of time restraints, Eugene hitched his chin toward the glove box.

Wiping the tears from her cheeks with the palm of her hand, Zoë slowly opened the glove box to retrieve her flashlight. As she lifted it from the compartment, she swung it at his head. He grabbed her hand and squeezed until she cringed and opened her fingers to release the flashlight.

"Please don't make me hurt you, Zoë," Eugene pleaded. "Punch would be very upset, and he's been good to me."

Rubbing her arm and her wrist, she retreated into her seat. "And this is how you repay him?"

"I'll be gone soon," Eugene said in as calm a manner as he could muster. "I just need you to help me get something, and then you'll be free to go home. In the meantime, sit back and be quiet. Please."

Hugging herself, Zoë flopped back against the seat and dropped her head back against the headrest.

Eugene pushed down hard on the accelerator. He was running out of time.

Clasping the side of a pickup truck, Punch dragged himself to a standing position. His head throbbed and his vision wobbled while nausea molested him. He could feel the warmth of his own blood sliding down the nape of his neck behind the collar of his shirt to dribble between his shoulder blades.

Oh yeah, Eugene had whacked him a good one.

The breeze felt good against his cheeks, and the spit of rain was like cold water hitting a hot pan. Though his vision was perverted, he could see his truck parked a few yards away. Staggering, he clung to vehicles while he made his way to his pickup. His feet felt like fifty pound weights. The fierce effort he put forth to keep conscious while he traveled forced him to his knees when he finally arrived at his pickup. He wretched onto the ground, and then sat back to muster the constitution to clamber to his feet and climb into his truck.

After what seemed like an eternity, he yanked the door open to fall across the seat. He was thankful that he was in the habit of keeping a bottle of water in the cup holder. Twisting the cap from the plastic bottle, he poured a bit over his head, and then gulped the rest down his throat. It was warm, but it was wet. His thoughts were jumbled, except for one: *Find Eugene. Bring Zoë back safely. And, if at all possible, beat the living shit out of Eugene.*

He gathered his thoughts together enough to reach into his pocket for his cell phone. He dialed Mike's number. "Hi, this is Mike West, I'm not available—" Punch pitched the phone to the passenger's seat and twisted the key in the ignition.

The rain started to fall steadily. It plunked hard against the windshield in fat droplets. Lightning sliced the night skies, and the thunder moaned like a wounded solider lying on a battlefield.

Yep, he was on his own. *Damned to hell.* Punch jammed the truck into *DRIVE* and spun out of the parking spot. The truck bounced and jerked while he drove through the vehicles at a high speed over the bumps and ruts. It made his head throb more and his stomach twist.

Shane stepped out from between two vehicles only to dive back among them to avoid being hit. "What the hell's up with him?"

~ THIRTEEN ~

"Okay, grab your favorite gal, cuz we're gonna slow it down a little," Butchie, the leader of the band announced into the mike. "I'd like to invite my beautiful niece, Taysa, on up here to sing for us." The crowd clapped and hollered while Taysa made her way to the make-shift stage.

The couples cuddled close together in anticipation of the slower music about to begin.

Lugowski led Ava onto the dance floor. He twirled her under his arm before pulling her in close to his chest. She smiled up at him. Unable to resist her green eyes he pressed his lips to hers. He didn't care who was looking. She was his. Laying her head against Lugowski's shoulder, Ava slipped her hands into the back pocket of his jeans to squeeze his buttocks while they swayed back and forth to Taysa's lovely voice.

With her bottom lip pinched between her teeth, she found herself searching the party for Kate and Holden. They weren't in the crowd. She hadn't seen them all evening. A tug of regret scraped through her for her outburst that revealed Holden's infidelity. She snuggled deeper into Lugowski's embrace to feel safe and hidden from her rashness.

Holden was struggling with an inner conflict that had something to do with Chip Walker. Ava and Doc Spears' investigation attempt that afternoon had come up empty.

She shouldn't have let Kate push her temper into overdrive. She should have held her tongue because when she thought about it, Kate West was good for Holden Reese. He was in love with her. Ava could see it in his eyes every time he looked at her.

Tears assaulted her eyes. What compelled her to hurt others? After all, she had someone who adored her—someone who would do anything for her—Carl. Why was it never quite enough? What was it that she was searching for? There was a driving force deep within her to control and manipulate the people and situations around her—especially when the people were men and the situations involved men.

Lugowski laid his cheek on the top of her head. She could feel the passion permeating from his embrace. He was a good man—a solid as a rock man. For that matter, if she was being truly honest, Mike West was a good man—rock solid. She had spent five years sabotaging that marriage—until he just couldn't take it anymore. Perhaps that was what she was about—testing men's limits. She lifted her face to look into Lugowski's eyes. *What's Carl's limit?*

Ava's deliberations were suddenly interrupted when a young man tapped Lugowski on the shoulder. "Lieutenant Lugowski?" he asked.

"Yeah?"

"There're three guys lying in the field. They're pretty beat up. Me and my friends found them on our way to our car," he said in an anxious voice.

Lugowski spotted Mike sitting on a bale of straw talking with Dan Quaide. Dragging Ava by the hand and with the young man at his heels, he picked through the crowd to reach them. "Where's McMinn and Strom?" he asked Mike.

"I don't know. I haven't seen him for twenty minutes or so." Mike stretched his neck to scan the party.

"Follow me," Lugowski said. "You, too, Mr. Quaide. I may need you to confirm some party guests." He turned to Ava. "Stay here." He spun to follow the young man out of the barn with Mike and Dan behind him.

The four men hastened down the ramp that bounced and creaked and gave beneath their feet. The young man led them through the dark field. They weaved through trucks and cars and SUVs while the rain pelted their faces until they could see the beam of a flashlight in the close distance between vehicles.

The young man's friends had Burke, Jay, and Chuck leaning against their car. They held their aching heads. Blinking their swelling bruised eyes, they tried to come to grips with their surroundings.

Lugowski flashed his badge. "What happened here?"

"They don't seem to want to tell us anything," a tall lanky young man said.

"You boys been fighting?" Lugowski asked.

"Yes, sir." Burke spit blood into the weeds.

"What about?"

Burke leaned his head against the car. The cool rain showered his swollen cheeks. He measured Lugowski and his badge through his swelling eyes. He tried to smile but it hurt too badly. "Just a little too much to drink and a little disagreement is all." Wincing in pain, he swallowed some blood. "I don't think that's against any laws, officer."

Lugowski shrugged. "Are you guests of Mr. Quaide?"

"Yes, sir."

Lugowski turned to Dan. "Do you know these boys, Mr. Quaide?"

Dan shook his head.

Lugowski nodded at Mike. "You?"

Mike shook his head.

Just then, Shane strolled up to the group. His brows furrowed while he studied the battered faces of the three men seated on the ground.

"What's your name?" Lugowski asked.

"Burke."

Shane and Mike exchanged telling glances. Shane stepped forward to stand next to Lugowski while Mike came to stand on the other side.

Shane said, "Ask him where Eugene Strom is, Lugowski, 'cause these are the guys who came to the farm the other night."

"Are you sure?" Lugowski asked. "You said it was too dark to get a look at them."

"Burke is the name Eugene gave for the man who came into the barn," Mike said. "He and two other guys had been chasing him down for months. By the looks of these guys, they must've caught up with him. Eugene used to be a fighter."

"I just saw Punch shoot outta here like a bat outta hell," Shane said. "Something's going down, and I'm betting it isn't good."

"In what direction did Punch go?" Mike asked.

"South." Shane nodded toward the road.

"I can't leave these guys," Lugowski said.

The burly horse trainer stepped forward and crossed his arms over his chest. Drops of rain dripped from his elbows. Dan said, "They ain't goin' anywhere, lieutenant. Believe me."

Lugowski slapped Dan on the back. "Oh, I believe it." He turned to Mike and Shane. "My cruiser is over there. Let's go."

The three of them dashed toward Lugowski's white SUV. The ground squished under their feet and rain dripped from their hair into their eyes.

Over a crash of thunder, Mike called out to Lugowski, "Why do I always get stuck with your sorry ass?"

Lugowski chuckled while yanking the driver's door open. "Just lucky I guess."

ॐ   ॐ   ॐ   ॐ

Eugene rolled Zoë's SUV to a stop alongside the dirt road. The rain danced in the headlights that lit up the marred tree where he had wrecked his car days ago. Leaving the headlights on, he turned the ignition off.

Zoë scooted toward the passenger's door. "Why are we stopping here?"

"We gotta get something." While shouldering the door open, he grabbed the flashlight and turned it on. "C'mon." He waited while she slipped out of the vehicle into the rain. Taking her by the hand, he led her across the road. Lighting the way with her flashlight, they traveled along the old rusting railroad tracks that disappeared into the tall weeds.

The sound of the water slapping over the rocks in Reardon's Run blended like an angry opus with the rain and the wind.

Baffled, Zoë pulled back. He turned to her. Her sopping hair stuck to her face, and her soaked dress sucked against her thighs. "Where are we going?" she yelled above the storm. "There's nothing over here but an old broken-down bridge."

"I need you to get something for me. You said that you weren't afraid of heights." He yanked her through the wet grasses to the boarded up entrance of the bridge. Gently, he took her by the waist and helped her over the blockade. "Careful now, there's a big hole, right..." He flashed the beams from the flashlight over the floor of the bridge. "—there."

Zoë inched her way around the huge gap in the boards. She grabbed the rusted railing with both hands. The wind whipped through the bridge. As hot as it had been for weeks, she now felt cold. Finally, Eugene joined her next to the railing.

"Okay, Zoë, here's what I need for you to do. I need you to climb down to that third beam." He flashed the light beneath the bridge.

Her spine stiffened. Her fingers curled around the railing until her knuckles turned white.

He continued with his instructions. "There's a package tied to it. I need you to bring me the package. Then, I promise I'll take you home."

Horrified, Zoë cried out, "Are you crazy? I can't climb down there!"

Eugene grabbed her by the shoulders. Looking intently into her eyes, he explained, "You said you weren't afraid of heights. Now, I'm gonna hold the light for you while you climb down—"

"Why don't you climb down there?" Zoë asked.

"I would, but I can't leave you up here to go get the police while I'm down there. I know it's terribly ungentlemanly of me, but you've gotta go."

The rain beat against her body. Looking over the railing into the dark abyss, hearing the thrashing water, Zoë shook with fear.

Lightning flashed and the thunder cracked.

Eugene flinched.

Wet and slippery, Zoë managed to slither from his grasp. She spun around to dart across the bridge to who knew where. She ran blindly into the darkness—anywhere to get away. The brittle boards gave under her sandals, and she wasn't sure if there was flooring all the way to the other end. She couldn't see the other end, but it had to be there somewhere in the blinding darkness! Her efforts were futile.

Eugene caught up, grabbed her by the arm, and whirled her around to face him.

Screaming, she beat him frantically with her fists. "No! I won't go!"

Dragging her back to the spot above where he had tied the package to the beam, he apologized. Yet his tone was brusque. "I'm sorry, Zoë, I know you're afraid, but you gotta go. Don't make me hurt you. If there was any other way I'd do it." He gave her a moment to collect herself. "I don't think you should try to climb down there with those sandals on. You'll slip, and I don't want you to fall."

Simpering, Zoë reached down, unfastened her sandals, and slipped them off.

In a softened tone, Eugene said, "Good girl. Now, nice and easy, I'll help you over the railing."

Zoë grabbed him by the front of his drenched shirt, "Before I do this... at least tell me what's in the package that I'm risking my life for."

"I owe you that. Money, a very large sum of money."

The rain pelting her face, she glowered at him. Accepting her fate, she grasped the railing and swung her right leg over. He steadied her while she lifted her left leg over. Staring down into the darkness, listening to the water crashing over the creek bed far below, she stood stark-still.

"What the fuck is going on?!" Punch's voice boomed across the bridge.

~ Fourteen ~

Eugene yanked the gun from his waistband. With unsteady hands, he kept it trained on Punch while he eased toward them at the very edge of the bridge.

Punch was filled with trepidation at the sight of Zoë clinging to the frail rusted railing. She shivered against the punishing rain and wind. Her sundress clung to every crevasse of her body. Her long hair lay in wet tangles about her shoulders and over her cheeks. Her teeth chattered.

Punch was within ten feet, when Eugene held his hand up. "Stay there, Punch, and keep your hands where I can see them."

Raising his hands, Punch complied. He nodded toward Zoë, whose legs wobbled. Her hands shook so fervently that the railing quaked. He didn't plead. He demanded politely, "Please let Zoë back on the bridge."

"Gladly," Eugene said, "I didn't want to send her down there in the first place."

"Down where?"

"Below to the third beam—where my money is tied-up in a waterproof sack."

Keeping the gun aimed at Punch, Eugene held out his arm for Zoë to grab to climb back over the rail onto the bridge.

The terror on her face did not diminish. She ran her harried hands through her soaking hair to brush it away from her face. Her lips quivered in her effort to control the hiccup of sobs that she wanted to set free.

Eugene gestured with the gun for Punch to approach the rail. "I guess you'll be doing the climbing, dude."

With measured steps and his head throbbing, Punch made his way toward the railing. "Then, what?"

"We'll discuss that when you come back up." Eugene flashed the beams of light over the bridge. He expelled a long downward whistle. "It's a long way down there."

Punch glared at him.

Eugene sighed. "I guess now is the time for the truth. I had just climbed up onto the edge when you showed up the other day. I was pretty shaken up. That's a damned scary climb even in the daylight, but I sure as hell wasn't gonna jump."

"What about the car?" Punch asked.

"I was in a hurry. I had lost Burke but I needed a good hiding place for the money real quick—somewhere that they would never even think of looking. I just took the turn on the road too fast, slid in the gravel, and the tree got in the way."

Another wave of nausea flooding over him, Punch gripped the railing. Trying to steady him, Zoë touched his shoulder gently. His voice was filled with a bitter tone. "So it was all a big act?"

"No... I really am a bad dancer," Eugene said, "and, I really didn't have the money. It was down there the whole time. No one ever asked me if I knew where the money was—only if I *had* the money."

Nostrils flared, Punch scowled at the man that he had helped because he thought he was desperate. He thought he was in trouble. He thought he could help him—*Punch McMinn, the Good*

Samaritan. Bullshit! Punch McMinn—the biggest idiot in the county! "Why didn't you just let me fall into the creek that day? Why did you pull me up?"

"I'm not a total prick, Punch," he said. "In fact, if Eric hadn't showed up the other day, I would've got the sack myself and been long gone. I wouldn't be asking you to do this if I weren't in dire straights. Could we please get on with it?"

Eugene motioned for Zoë to step away from Punch. Tentatively, she did as she was instructed.

Punch wiped what rain he could from his face, and then swung his right leg over the railing, followed by his left. Squatting down, he grabbed the thick steel girder and wrapped his legs around it. He slid down about five or six feet. The sliding came easy down the wet steel. Holding on tightly, he found purchase with his left foot on a crossbeam where he hesitated to swallow down the nausea and dizziness.

The rushing water below clapped against the rocks. Although he couldn't see it, he knew exactly how far the fall would be to his certain death. Lightning sliced the sky while Punch crawled along the junction of beams to the next.

The vertigo and nausea wouldn't let up, but his irritation heightened. "I need more light, ass wipe!" he hollered.

Eugene shone the beams toward his voice, except the flashlight wasn't of the grade to provide much more than a small amount of illumination. "That's as good as it gets, I'm afraid." Eugene sounded almost apologetic—but not really.

Huffing from the nausea, dizziness, and angst; Punch wrapped his body around the next beam. It was difficult to get a good grip on the wet slippery metal. The rain fell down his forehead to irritate his eyes—not that he could see, but he couldn't afford to wipe the water away either.

He slid to the next crossbeam more quickly. It was a scary ride. He wasn't sure that he would stop this time, or that he would come to a crossbeam, but suddenly his body jerked to a stop when his behind slammed against it. The impact jolted the pain from one end of his body to the other.

Resting his aching forehead against the beam that he clung to, he took a moment to collect himself. The cool rain struck him like pea gravel mixing with the sweat dribbling down his temples.

Panic rolled through him at the thought that perhaps he'd veered off course during his descent, and he wasn't as close to the package as he had thought.

Closing his eyes, he felt himself slipping into a welcomed state of nothingness. His shoulders slumped, and his hands slipped down the beam onto his thighs. The wooziness from his head injury lured him within a whisper of sweet oblivion when Eugene's voice jerked him back into the moment. "Are you okay down there, big guy?"

Feeling the sudden sensation of slipping from his seated position, Punch's chin hitched upward. His eyes blinked open only to have the rain assault them. Consciousness of his precarious position swept over him. Both of his big hands clutched the beam. "Yeah, yeah, I'm okay," he said. "How much farther?"

"Reach above your head. It should be tied to the crossbeam, if you're low enough."

"Why'd you come down so freakin' far, asshole?"

"I was makin' sure, is all," Eugene said. "Didn't think I'd have to come back for it on a dark rainy night. Is it there?"

Punch reached over his head to feel along the beams—nothing but rusting, flaking steel. Damn, he would have to go down yet another level.

That's when the dreaded thought hit him, *What if it had come untied and had fallen into Reardon's Run? What if the money's gone? What can I expect from this man that I'd tried to help, who has betrayed me?* He didn't care what Eugene did to him, but what would he do to Zoë? He shoved the thought aside. No, Eugene wouldn't climb down all this way only not to fasten the package good and tight. He couldn't afford negative thoughts. He would never make it back to the bridge if he let them devour his mind. It would be there. Yes, the money sack would be there when he got to the correct beam.

Punch climbed to the next beam, wrapped his leg around it, and let his body slide to the next juncture. He hoped it was the one that he was searching blindly in the dark for. Anticipating the crossbeam, his foot found purchase.

Painstakingly, he straddled the crossbeam while reaching over his head to feel along the wet flaking steel for the package. The rope pricked his fingers. He let out the breath he'd been holding. It cleansed his lungs of at least a little anguish.

"Found it," he called out.

"Good!" Eugene's voice boomed from the bridge.

"Thank God," he heard Zoë say through a whimper.

Lightning lit up the sky once more to illuminate the package above him. It confirmed that he indeed had found what he had risked the deadly descent for.

With his hand, he took a swing at the rope's tie—missing it. Involuntarily, he began to laugh. He couldn't smother the laugh. It was idiotic, but he couldn't stop. "What if I drop it?" he called out through his senseless chortling.

From the bridge, Eugene shook his head at the question. "That would be really bad for Zoë."

Punch's voice echoed from below. "And if I bring it up?"

Eugene glanced at Zoë's exhausted, soaked to the skin, and wary expression. "I'll take Zoë's car and leave you two to walk back to the party."

"I've got your word?"

"Seriously?" Eugene asked. "Does that really mean anything to you at this point?"

"It's gotta, Eugene. It's just gotta."

Eugene let out a long sigh. "For what it's worth... You've got my word, Punch."

Wiping the rain and the sweat from his face, Punch stretched to untie the package. Carefully, he eased the package from its hiding place and shoved the rope between his teeth to begin his treacherous climb to the bridge—only he'd lost track of his route. He would have to make the climb feeling his way along the beams—not sure where he would surface.

"I keep getting his voice mail," Mike said.

The flame of his Butane lighter lit-up Lugowski's face as he drew it to the cigarette he'd just stuck in his mouth. He asked, "How long ago did he call you?" He steered the SUV along the gravel road. The windshield wipers swept the rain from the glass. The headlights illuminated the trees swaying like sinewy monsters in the darkness above the road.

The screen from his cell phone lit up Mike's face while he scrolled through his missed calls. "About a half-hour ago. They could be on any one of these back roads. Eugene's definitely on the run. But why is he running from Punch? If he's on the run, what's he capable of?"

"My experience is that desperate people will do a shit load of crazy things—including kill someone trying to help them." Lugowski blew smoke from his nostrils. "Is Strom armed?"

"Who knows?" Mike replied.

Shining the flashlight through the broken board in the bridge floor that Punch had fallen through days ago, Eugene watched Punch heave and slip while he climbed upward with the package between his teeth. "You're almost there!" he called down to Punch.

Pressing her hand against her chest, Zoë squeezed her eyes shut in relief that Punch would soon be on the bridge—safe and sound with her. Eugene would have his money. She would be more than willing to let him have her SUV. Unable to locate her sandals, her feet were sore from splinters buried in her skin. Regardless, she would be happy to walk several miles in the pouring rain back to the party with sore or bleeding feet as long as Punch was safe. Surely, this man would keep his word and let them go. She blew out a breath of pure relief when Punch's hands emerged through the hole in the floor of the bridge and his head popped through.

"Good job! You got a little off-course coming back, but you're up all the same." Eugene rushed from the railing toward the hole in the floor and reached for the package.

Only Punch grabbed the rope from between his teeth. Using it like a lasso he whacked Eugene in the face.

Eugene fell backward to the bridge floor while Punch quickly hoisted himself through the hole. Eugene was managing to crawl to his feet when Punch dove on top of him to knock the gun from his hand. The gun exploded while it spun and bounced in circles across the splintered decking until it came to a stop at Zoë's feet.

~ Fifteen ~

Lugowski rolled the SUV to a stop at an intersection of three desolate roads. Taking in another drag from the cigarette, he looked to the right, and then to the left. "Which way, gentlemen?"

"They could've gone anywhere," Mike said. "In this blasted rain, we can't even track them through a dust cloud."

A nanosecond later, a gunshot rang out through the storm.

Momentarily frozen, they exchanged wary glances.

"Shit!" Mike yelled. "Someone's definitely armed. Turn right, Lugowski, I think it came from the old bridge."

Lugowski spun the steering wheel to the right and pressed his foot hard to the accelerator. The SUV fish-tailed in the gravel while he grabbed the mike to his radio and pressed it to his mouth. "Shots fired at the old railroad bridge on Reardon's Road. Need back-up and an ambulance."

Punch wasted no time. He wrapped his fingers around Eugene's neck and squeezed with all his might. Eugene's strength was a fierce match for the huge man. He managed to bring his arms up between Punch's. His strong hands separated Punch's arms. Double fisted, he slammed Punch in the jaw to send him backward to the floor.

In the darkness, Zoë fell to her knees. The gun had bounced in her direction, but she couldn't see it. The rough jagged planking stabbed into her skin while she felt along the boards in her mad search for the weapon.

She jerked back with a yelp when a splinter spiked under her fingernail. Drawing her finger to her lips, the acrid taste of her blood mixed with filth filled her mouth. Panting, Zoë pressed on crawling along the floor. The rain pounded on her back and flowed through her hair. Her knee scraped along the rusted remnants of the train track. She jerked when the old corroded screws ripped her skin. The blood rippled along her legs to mix with the dirt and the water pooling on the saturated planking. Ignoring the burning pain, she continued her quest for the gun.

She had to find it.

She wasn't sure that she could use it once it was found. It was so wickedly dark, that if she should dare take a shot, she could wound or possibly kill the wrong man. While she scrounged along the abrasive boards, she had to consider if she was capable of shooting at another human being.

His head throbbing even harder, and the nausea sweeping through him, Punch attempted to push to his feet, but the street fighter was prepared for any scenario. He kicked Punch hard in the gut.

Eugene purposely avoided contact with his head. He knew that he'd already injured Punch badly when he hit him with the butt of his gun. He didn't want to kill Punch. The man didn't deserve that from him. He only wanted to incapacitate him so that he could escape with the money, and Zoë's vehicle. He hated the thought that he might need to drag Zoë along as a hostage, but it was quickly becoming the viable option.

Eugene searched the bridge for the gun. It was too dark. He couldn't see it, or the money sack. He could only see the outline of Zoë crawling along the floor. She was looking for the gun, too. He had to get to it before she did!

Finally, Zoë's fingers bumped into the gun. Shaking, she picked it up while trying to see through the darkness.

Thunder cracked and lightning lit the sky. For a nanosecond, she could see the flicker of the loaded weapon in her hands, and the huge mass of the man watching her while she knelt clutching the gun to her chest. The lightning illuminated the sharp planes of his face and flashed the desperation in his eyes only a few feet away.

The world spun around him in the darkness while Punch struggled to stand. His head throbbed like violent thunderheads in his brain. His eyes refused to focus. His hand felt along the planking until they came upon the toe of Eugene's boot. Swiftly, his fingers crawled up his foot until reaching the ankle. Grabbing hold, he pulled with what might he had left.

Eugene slammed to the floor with a loud grunt to knock the wind out of him. Punch did his best to scramble to his feet.

But, by the time he stood, Eugene had recovered.

"Is that you, Punch?" Zoë called into the dark. Extending the gun out in front of her with trembling hands, she fingered the trigger while trying to decide whether to pull it. Mustering the courage to shoot the man who was advancing toward her, she swallowed hard.

For Punch, her words seemed far away on the other side of consciousness. He blinked his eyes while trying to hear her more clearly.

Wrapping her quivering finger around the trigger, she cried out, "Who's there?"

Punch tried to answer, but nothing came from his mouth.

Eugene grabbed him from behind in a bear hug and lifted him from his feet. "C'mon Punch! Why won't you stay down? I don't want to hurt you anymore than you are! Just stay down!" Eugene pleaded into his ear.

Stay down? Was he kidding? This man had used Punch's good intentions to buy time until he could figure a plan to escape with the dirty money that he claimed he didn't have. Worse, he dragged Zoë to this bridge and was going to make her climb down that death trap for his goddamned money! No way in hell was he going to stay down.

With his last spark of awareness, he enveloped his arms around Eugene's and with the last bit of his strength that he could muster; he hurled Eugene over his shoulders. Eugene's body crashed through the hole in the bridge floor. Listening to Eugene's screams as he fell, and finally the sound of his body smashing into the fast waters of Reardon's Run, Punch dropped to his knees.

Everything went black...

The headlights of the SUV fell upon Zoë's white Outlander and Punch's red pickup parked at the side of the road. Lugowski reached under his seat for his Glock and a flashlight. Tossing the used-up cigarette out the window, he turned to Mike. "You two stay low and behind me. I can't afford to get anyone shot-up."

"What?" Mike asked. "You're not going to make us sit in the car?"

"Would you?"

"No."

"That's what I thought. Let's go." They clambered out of the vehicle into the dark and rain. Staying low, they jogged across the road and into the tall grass to make their way toward the old bridge.

Punch could barely hold on to consciousness, yet he could hear Zoë's whimpers. Laboriously, he pulled himself up to stumble toward the faraway sound.

Gulping for air in between sobs, Zoë still held the gun in her outstretched hand. She could hear the footsteps approaching her. She could make out a huge shadow coming at her. The figure was back-splashed by the infrequent lightning. Eyes wide with fright, the gun shook in her hand.

"It's okay, Zoë. It's me." Punch's throat was dry and his voice was raspy.

The lightning spiked to glint off the barrel of the gun. He extended his hand out to her. "Give me the gun, baby, everything's okay."

Pointing the gun at him as he made his way closer, she remained frozen in place.

Finally, he stood before her. Carefully, he took the gun from her hand and dropped it to the floor. Sobbing, she fell against his chest. He folded her in his arms and dropped his cheek on the top of her head. She clutched his soaked shirt. The water squished through her fingers. She shivered in his arms like it was thirty degrees instead of eighty.

Zoë was safe, and for that he was so very thankful.

Punch's heart felt heavy for the man who had fallen to his death in the fast waters beneath the bridge. Only five days ago, he had found him with desperation etched on his face and clinging to the railing.

It was the same desperation that became his demise. Oblivion called to him. Oh, how he wanted to close his eyes and let it guide him to the quiet void that it promised. Allowing his lids to drop, he took a chance. Growing weaker, his knees wobbled.

A beam of light sliced through the barricade at the end of the bridge.

Zoë gasped.

Lugowski called out, "McMinn, is that you?"

Punch was too exhausted to answer. His body trembled.

"We need help!" Zoë answered. She could see three figures climbing over the barricade. "Watch the hole in the road!"

Shooting the beams in front of them, Lugowski carefully stepped around the hole. The three men made their way toward Punch and Zoë.

"Where's Strom?" Lugowski asked.

"He's floating in the creek." Punch suddenly put all his weight onto Zoë.

"He's hurt! Eugene hit him in the head with his gun!" Knowing she couldn't hold him, she felt his weight upon her.

Jumping forward, Mike and Shane grabbed their friend to hold him up. Lugowski rushed to the railing and flashed the beams from his light into the waters.

The swift current loosened Eugene's body from a rock that he was slumped over to carry his broken lifeless body into the darkness.

With a solemn shake of his head, Lugowski directed his beam toward Mike and Shane who were lowering Punch to a sitting position. They bent their bodies over him to shield him from the unrelenting rain.

Mike examined the gash on the back of his head, while asking him questions: "What's your name?" Punch mumbled something. "What's your address?" Again Punch responded with an unintelligible mumble. Mike was afraid to allow him to close his eyes. He gently tapped Punch's face. "C'mon Punch, stay with me. Stay with me, buddy."

Searching the deck of the bridge, Lugowski's flashlight settled on a package a short distance from where they had seated Punch. With marked steps around the huge hole, he made his way to the sack and picked it up by the rope with the tips of his fingers. He wasn't exactly sure why he was being so careful with the evidence. The rain was washing away all the fingerprints or DNA that the lab could've collected anyway. It was mechanical on his part to handle evidence with caution, even evidence that had been compromised.

"It's full of money," Zoë said to the lieutenant through chattering teeth. "I don't know when, but Eugene hid it below the bridge. He forced Punch to climb down to get it. I was so afraid he'd fall." She cupped her hand over her mouth to stifle the anxiety that still gripped her.

Mike patted Punch on the back, and then stood up. He wrapped his arms around her to transfer any warmth his rain-soaked body could provide. "C'mon, Zoë, I'll take you to your car until the ambulance gets here. We'll get you out of this rain and maybe warm you up a bit."

"What about Punch?" she asked.

"I don't think we should move him right now," Mike said. "I'm not sure we could move him. Don't worry, Shane will stay with him." He urged her forward in his embrace.

She hesitated. Then, by Lugowski's flashlight, she let Mike lead her past the hole in the road bed and through the barricade at the end of the bridge.

Through half-lidded eyes, Punch watched Mike lead Zoë away. He was glad that she would soon be dry and warm.

Once Lugowski saw that Mike had taken Zoë to safety, he knelt next to Punch and Shane. He shined the flashlight on the sack that dangled between his fingers. "Is this the money from the fight?"

Shane placed an arm around Punch. "Back-off, Lugowski. He's not in any shape to interrogate. There's no way Punch knew that Eugene had the money."

"How do you know that?" Lugowski asked.

"Because I know Punch," Shane said. "He helped Eugene because he needed help, but he would never condone stealing money, and that's a fact."

Sirens wailed in the distance.

Lugowski said, "While I appreciate you defending your friend, I will question him at length once he's seen a doctor, and for his sake, I hope you're right."

~ SIXTEEN ~

Punch didn't want to open his eyes. He preferred the deep relaxed state of sleep that kept the throb to a minimum. The voices around him urged him awake. His lids fluttered open to an out of focus room with bright lights, and a woman standing over him dressed in blue scrubs. He squinted and strained until she finally came into focus.

The nurse adjusted an IV bag, and then glanced down at him. She smiled. "Hello Mr. McMinn," she said in a soft tone. "We stitched up that nasty gash on your head. You suffered a concussion. You'll probably have a headache for several days, and you may experience some dizziness now and then. If you take it easy, you should be fine in a couple of weeks."

She looked over her shoulder. "He's awake, Mr. West." She walked toward the door. "If there's anything I can get him, please call."

"Thank you." Mike pulled a chair up next to the bed. "How you feeling, big guy?"

Turning his head, Punch grimaced. "Like I've been hit over the head. How long have I been out?"

"Couple hours."

"Is Zoë okay?"

"She was pretty shook-up, but she wasn't hurt. She wasn't happy, but I had Shane drive her home before she got sick. She was soaked to the skin and shaking. Lugowski took her statement. He's waiting to talk with you. I can tell him to shove off until tomorrow if you want."

"Bring it," Punch said.

"Good," Lugowski said from the doorway. "The doctor just informed me that they're releasing you, so you're obviously well enough for a talk."

Mike jerked from his chair. His jaw was tight. "Are you freakin' kidding me, Lugowski? You know damned well that Punch didn't have anything to do with that missing money. Why aren't you questioning those three goons that had been following Eugene for months?"

"They're tight lipped, lawyered-up, and I've got a strong feeling that they'll be free on bail by tomorrow morning," Lugowski told him. "That said, they're suggesting that Punch was hiding Eugene out for a portion of the money, only Eugene got greedy in the end. Zoë confirmed that Eugene split your head open, tried to force her to retrieve the money, and then when you showed up made you go instead. I stuck around to make sure you were okay, and to let you know that you're in the clear, McMinn."

He turned to Mike. "Take him home, and make sure he gets plenty of rest."

Mike let out a breath of relief. "Will do. Thanks, man."

Lugowski added before he stepped out of the room. "I'll stop by the farm tomorrow for a full statement."

Doc Spears wasn't in the habit of sitting in his truck on a desolate dirt road at two o'clock in the morning for a rendezvous. He was usually home, snug in his bed, sawing logs; but this was important. He couldn't let Chip Walker and Holden Reese get away with drugging horses. It went against everything he stood for.

Kate would be heartbroken, and for that he was sorry. Her feelings were the only thing that gave him pause for what he was about to do—what he had to do.

While tapping his crooked fingers on the steering wheel, a set of headlights flashing in his rear-view mirror caught his attention. This was it. The car slowed and parked behind his vet truck. His right hand shifted from the steering wheel to his shirt pocket. The paper crinkled inside the pocket while he fingered it nervously.

He watched in his mirror as the detective slid from his car. With his gun drawn, he approached Doc's truck with caution. Doc let his window down and made sure his hands were in plain sight at all times when the detective pointed the gun through the window. "Dr. Ben Spears?" he asked.

"Yes, sir," Doc replied.

"Please get out of the vehicle slowly, sir."

Doc complied.

The detective looked inside his truck to ensure he was alone. He then patted Doc down quickly. Satisfied, he motioned him toward his vehicle with his gun. Doc hobbled to the passenger's side of the cruiser. The detective opened the door and Doc got in. Scanning the area, the detective made his way around the car. He slid into the driver's seat and closed the door.

"Dr. Benjamin Spears: head veterinarian at the Keystone Downs Racetrack for almost forty years, graduated out of Ohio State University, no criminal record other than a parking ticket on Fifth Street in Rosemount in 1985, and a speeding ticket on Route 224 in 1998—"

"I wasn't speeding," Doc said. "That's a fifty-five mile per hour zone. The officer didn't know what he was talking about."

Looking down at a file, the detective raised his eyebrows. "Says here in my report that you paid a one-hundred-twenty dollar fine."

"I was too busy to fight the charge," Doc said.

The detective rolled his eyes. "Okay. My name's Jack Haliday. Surely, we're not here to discuss an old speeding ticket."

Doc pulled a prescription slip from his shirt pocket and held it out to the detective.

Jack eyed the paper and the old man. He slipped on a pair of latex gloves while asking, "How did you retrieve this evidence, sir?"

"It fell out of Chip Walker's pocket. It was in plain view. I picked it up. If I had gone into his office without him knowing that would be breaking and entering. That's against the law."

"That's correct, Dr. Spears. So my understanding is that you found this on the ground."

"Something like that. Look, he's drugging horses with this young vet's help. Horses that haven't won a race in ages are winning big purses—impressively. They're getting the horses through the drug screening somehow. There needs to be an investigation. They need to be stopped."

Jack studied the prescription. "I didn't know that veterinarians could write prescriptions."

"We can, but it's most unusual. You'd think a pharmacist would question the large dosage recommended on the script."

Jack was taken aback when he noticed the dosage—ten times what a human would require. "Unless he doesn't."

"That's exactly right, detective."

~ SEVENTEEN ~

Punch slept most of the day away. He woke with a start when Bart jumped from who knows where onto his pillow next to his face. The tomcat sidled up close to knead Punch's shoulder with his paws.

Rubbing his head, Punch was most pleased that the throb had subsided to a dull thump. He was glad to be waking in his own bed in his own apartment. Mike wanted him to spend the night at his place in the spare bedroom, but Punch insisted upon being taken home.

Mike complied with narrowed eyes and his forehead creased in concern. It was the exact same expression he wore when Punch arrived at Westwood in the afternoon to saddle up Charlatan. "I don't think you should be out riding a horse with a fresh head injury." Mike sounded like an old mother hen when he saw Punch toss the saddle onto Charlatan's back.

Punch appreciated Mike's apprehension, except sitting in his saddle on a beautiful Sunday afternoon, listening to the leather creak, while riding a good horse was the best medicine that he could think of.

If anything else, it would speed up the healing process, and it wasn't just the concussion that needed healing.

He and Charlatan made their way down the winding path that led to the training track. Beneath Charlatan's feet, the tall grasses seemed to be at ease after the rain had provided a good drink. Soon, the horse and rider dipped into the wooded section of Westwood that had been untouched. The trees provided a tangled canopy above their heads that blocked out most of the sun. Only slivers of its rays shown through. The layers of leaves from seasons before crunched under Charlatan's hooves while squirrels dashed from tree to tree. The large ground foliage flicked back and forth where the little creatures pounced over and under it. The air was cooler in the shadows of the trees. It was Mother Nature's air conditioning, and Punch welcomed the coolness and the scenery she presented so eloquently.

Charlatan's head hung low as if he were enjoying the easy stroll through the woods just as much as Punch. His head lifted and he snorted.

Punch pulled back on the reins to bring the gelding to a halt. His eyes narrowed. He heard the sound of footsteps crunching on twigs and leaves. Punch turned. His shoulders drooped and he shook his head. "Really, Sheldon? Really?" He moaned, when his eyes fell upon the colt following along. "Mike's gonna have a cow." He sighed, "Oh well, c'mon, I'm not turning back now. You may as well follow along."

Punch reined Charlatan forward through the brush and the trees until they spilled out onto a dirt road. Charlatan's shoes crunched along the gravel. Sheldon merrily followed along while stopping to check out the grass or nip at Charlatan's rump. Charlatan would swipe his tail in objection at the youngster, and Punch would laugh.

The sound of water slapping hard against the rocks filled Punch's ears—Reardon's Run. They walked along the road until they came to the railroad tracks that cut across just beyond the scarred tree where Eugene had rammed his car. Scrubbing his fingers across his face, he pulled Charlatan up to take a moment to stare at the tree. Sheldon munched the grass alongside the road.

Punch's eyes followed the tracks until they disappeared into the once tall grass that was now smashed into the ground where the police trampled through to investigate the scene, and remove Eugene's body from the creek.

Punch stepped down from the saddle. He wrapped the reins around the tree to secure Charlatan. With measured steps, he made his way toward the freshly tromped pathway that led to the old railroad bridge. Regret pinched his heart when his gaze fell upon the bright yellow crime scene tape that stretched across the barricade at the entrance of the bridge. He climbed over the tape and the boards until his feet found purchase on the splintered planking. His eyes immediately went to the large hole that he had fallen through a week ago, the same hole he had flung Eugene through to his death. The police had nailed some boards over it. Good idea.

Letting out a long sigh, he made his way to the railing.

Looking over the edge, the water pounded over the rocks with furious rhythm. The white caps swirled and popped in a vibrant choreography. He didn't have to close his eyes to remember the sight of Eugene clinging to the railing as if he were contemplating jumping.

Yes, he could see Zoë clinging to the same railing in the dark, terrified of what she was about to do. Thank, God, he got to the bridge in time. It could have been Zoë floating down the creek.

A loud cawing sound jerked him from his funk. He looked up into the crystal blue skies. The red-tailed hawk glided above the bridge with two youngsters circling her. She called to them and them to her. She dipped and swooped past the railing. Punch caught a glimpse of her magnificent colors and her amazing wingspan.

Nodding in silent appreciation, he watched the hawk and her young-ones fly beyond the trees. It was as if she knew he had been waiting ever so patiently to see them, and she was rewarding him for his patience.

Punch pushed away from the railing to make his way across the bridge and over the barricade. He walked through the smashed grass to the road before coming to a dead stop.

The horse's heads were up and their necks were arched. Snorting and punching at the ground with his right front hoof, Sheldon inched his way past Charlatan.

Slowly, Punch made his way toward the horses and whatever was causing them concern. His face lit up and he smiled. "Well, would ya look at that!"

❧ ❧ ❧ ❧

The day was getting old when Punch rode toward the barn with Sheldon lagging a short way behind. His nostrils still flared, he kept his distance from Charlatan.

Leaning against the wall with his arms crossed over his chest, Mike filled the barn's doorway. "I was getting really worried. I just got off the phone with Coco Beardmore. She said that she was more than willing to send a van for Charlatan. She even apologized for sending him here without talking to me first."

Punch patted Charlatan's shoulder. He braced himself for what Mike was about to tell him. He was almost afraid to ask, "What did you tell her?"

The left side of Mike's mouth lifted, "I told her Charlie fits in just fine. I think he's found a home here at Westwood."

Relieved, Punch smiled. "Good." Just then a *Baaaa* sounded from behind Charlatan. Mike straightened from the wall. His face tightened. Punch tugged on a piece of rope and a Billy goat appeared beside Charlatan. Sheldon snorted and then trotted past Charlatan and Mike to get into the barn.

"What the hell is that?" Mike asked in a high-pitched voice.

"What's it look like?"

"It looks like a damned goat!" Mike said.

"Yep. I found him on Reardon's Road. Somebody dumped the poor guy."

"We don't need a goat, Punch."

"I figured he'd make a great stable mate for Sheldon," Punch said.

"No!"

"Goats are supposed to be great stable companions for nervous horses—"

"No!"

"C'mon, Mike, just give him a try. He seems like a really nice goat—"

"I hate goats!"

"He's a perfectly good goat."

"There's no such thing!" Mike stomped into the barn.

Punch stepped off Charlatan to follow Mike into the barn while dragging the goat and Charlatan behind him. "Awe, c'mon, Mike..."

~ Epilogue ~

Jen eased through the front door with an armful of groceries. She thought it would be nice to surprise Eric and his family with a big Sunday dinner.

Making her way through the foyer toward the kitchen, she caught the scent of lavender filling the downstairs. She noticed the gentle glow of candle light in the study. Then she saw Kate's hair swept across the top of the sofa, and her bare feet propped on the coffee table. Her right ankle was crossed over her left. The right side of Jen's lips kicked up. Evidently, Eric wasn't in the house.

She set the bags of groceries on the stairs. Quietly, she approached the sofa.

Kate's hands were folded over her tummy while she absently fingered the pages of a book. She looked troubled.

Jen slowly lowered onto the sofa next to her. She whispered, "Penny for your thoughts?"

Kate expelled a slight laugh. "I don't know what to think."

"We missed you and Holden at the dance last night."

Tossing the book aside, Kate dragged her gaze to Jen. "Holden slept with Ava." There, she said it.

It was okay, because she trusted Jen. The woman reminded her of her mom. She wished her mom were here right now to give her some much-needed motherly advice. Yes, Kate was a grown woman of twenty-six, but hey some times a girl needs her mom. Jen had become someone she could confide in. She was so thankful for that.

Pursing her lips, Jen lifted her chin. She took a moment to weigh her response. "What are you going to do?"

Kate lifted both of her hands to her head and ran her fingers through her hair. She stopped at the nape of her neck and let go of an exasperated sigh. "Holden and I spent the entire night in an all night diner in Rosemount—talking. She did what Ava does so well—manipulate men. I want to strangle that bitch. Too bad that isn't an option. But telling Carl Lugowski is."

Jen favored her with a smile. She brushed back a frock of Kate's hair from her brows. "You want to hurt her back. I understand completely. About seven years ago, I had a good friend whose husband was cheating on her. I wanted to tell her, but my mother stopped me. She said, *Do you want to be responsible for your friend's divorce? Do you want to be responsible for her unhappiness? She'll find out on her own—if she doesn't already know. And then she can turn to you for the support she's going to need, instead of turning away from you because you ripped away her safety net. Many times that's what ignorance is: a safety mechanism.'*

Jen sighed. "Mom was right. My friend found out about his affairs a week later. I think Mom was right about the fact that she already knew, but didn't want to face it. So, you have to ask yourself: Do I want to be responsible for Carl's unhappiness?"

There it was—the motherly advice that she knew Jen would adeptly offer.

Kate covered her eyes with her palms. She could feel the heat of her tears wanting to surge to the surface. "Why isn't there any justice when it comes to Ava?"

Jen murmured, "What goes around comes around... eventually."

Kate dropped her hands to the cushions on the sofa and frowned at her.

Letting go of a tiny giggle, Jen smiled. "I know, it's an overused cliché, but I've found there's a lot of truth to it."

Kate pushed up from the sofa and slipped her feet into her sandals.

"Where are you going?" Jen asked.

"I need to think. I'm going for a drive."

❦　❧　❦　❧

The quiet felt good. His head still ached, and it was lonely; but Punch was used to evenings in his apartment alone with his TV and Bart. Mike and Shane had offered to come over for the evening with a pizza and beer to keep him company. They were like his brothers—no, they were his brothers. They were worried about his concussion and his state of mind, because that's what family does—worry. He told them that his head was aching, and that he was going to turn-in early.

The truth was that he simply wanted quiet. Sometimes the quiet and the loneliness was his solace. Solace. It was definitely what he was searching for following the disastrous debacle with Eugene Strom.

Hey, maybe I should wise-up or toughen-up. Maybe I should let humanity take care of itself instead of always trying to help out the other guy. It sure as hell doesn't seem to be working out. My brother's keeper—bullshit.

After taking a hot shower, he made some popcorn in the microwave, and sank into the sofa to fire-up the TV in hopes of something good on HBO—something to distract him from thoughts of Eugene's body falling from the bridge into Reardon's Run, and then floating broken down stream. He needed something to distract him from the memory of the terror in Zoë's eyes, and the tremble of her body against his in the aftermath. He would have done anything to shield her from what Eugene had put upon her.

Seemingly coming out of nowhere, Bart jumped onto the couch to make himself comfortable deep in the cushions behind Punch's head. The cat snuggling down for the evening urged a smile from the big man. "Hey Bart, you're facing the wrong way, dude. You're not gonna be able to see the TV."

The old tomcat mewed and buried his head into his paws.

"Well, okay then, I'll wake ya if there's anything good on."

He had just tossed a fistful of popcorn into his mouth when there was a knock on the door. A kernel slipped from the group landing on his still moist chest.

HBO was featuring *The Hunger Games.*

He considered ignoring the knock. He imagined that it was more than likely the sweet old woman, Mrs. Williams, from next door with a container of cookies.

The second round of knocks was a bit more insistent and accompanied by a familiar voice calling through the door, "Punch... are you in there? It's me, Zoë. I'd really like to talk to you."

He froze mid-chomp. Quickly, he switched off the TV and set the plastic bowl of popcorn onto the coffee table. Regret rolled through him. How was he going to politely tell her to get lost? Hurting Zoë was the last thing he ever want to do. It was best. He simply was not good enough for the likes of Zoë Miller. She should have a business man, not some guy that made a living looking after Thoroughbreds, a man with rough calloused hands, and a simple associates degree from the community college that he obviously was not using. Zoë deserved better.

Barefooted, he padded across his apartment. Sucking in a deep breath, he opened the door.

Zoë was turned away as if she were about to leave. Turning toward him, her big blue eyes drank him in. She was taken aback by the fact that he was shirtless, and the solitary kernel of popcorn clinging to his dark chest hair. Her lips parted. A tiny sigh escaped her.

Punch knew that a terse tone was appropriate for the task at hand: scaring her off. Yet one look into those sweet eyes brought him to the reality that he could never be terse with this woman—not with the feelings that ran deep into his soul. "Zoë, what are you doing here?"

She murmured, "We should talk."

Leaning against the jamb, he folded his arms over his chest. It was his best defense, his best effort at firm. "This can't happen, Zoë. It just can't."

Cocking her head to the side, she looked deeply wounded. "Why?"

Taking in a deep breath, he spread his arms out palming each side of the jamb as if hanging on a cross, crucified by what he was denying.

She was overcome by his sheer mass. She wanted to wrap her arms around this gentle giant of a man to show him the kind of love that she had to offer. Except Punch's apprehension stretched between them like a hot-wired chain-linked fence screaming, *Don't touch or you'll get burned!* Zoë wanted to get burned—good and burned.

"I'm black and you're white," Punch said.

Zoë's expression flooded with irritation. "That's all you've got?"

"That makes it complicated enough."

"For who? You or me?"

Damn this is hard. "For both of us," he said, "but mainly for you."

Her watery eyes grew wider still. Her irritation swelled into full-blown agitation. Zoë was having no problem pulling off a terse tone. "How dare you, Punch McMinn! How dare you decide what's best for me. I'm not some teen-aged white girl with a crush on the only black boy in school! I'm a full-grown intelligent woman who has been in love with a compassionate, sweet man since I laid eyes on him!"

"I'm not good enough for you, Zoë! You should be with someone with a big career and a big portfolio—"

"A white man in a stuffed shirt? That's who you think I belong with? Well, wouldn't that be freakin' grand?" In one quick sweep, she ducked under his arms and slipped into his apartment.

Punch was surprised by her nimble maneuver.

"You tell him, girl!" a sassy little voice called out from the apartment next door.

Punch glanced over to see the tiny old woman from the next apartment, Mrs. Williams, peeking over the security chain through the open gap in her door. Upon Punch's scolding look, she promptly slammed the door.

Reverently, he stepped into his apartment and closed the door behind him. He had visions of Mrs. Williams scampering to press her ear to wall.

Zoë held her ground. He couldn't help but think how hot she looked in her white sleeveless blouse and red floral skirt. Her dark blond locks drifted about her shoulders. Furthermore her expression was steadfast.

Planting her hands on her hips, she stated, "Let's get one thing straight, McMinn, I'll decide what's best for me." With that she snatched the kernel of popcorn from his chest and tossed it into her mouth.

Punch blinked back. *Shit, how can I argue my case now? There is no case.* She had effectively eradicated it, leaving him with only the submission to the feelings he'd been afraid to openly claim.

Crossing her arms under her breasts, Zoë was not-so-patiently waiting for his response. Moreover he had the feeling that it had better be good.

Okay, he had deep feelings for this lovely woman. Time to man-up, McMinn. What's it gonna hurt to explore a relationship? Besides, when one's in a relationship there are bound to be disagreements, by the looks of Zoë Miller at this moment, make-up sex would probably be hot, scorching hot.

The corners of his mouth slowly kicked up. "Would you like some popcorn?"

Relieved, Zoë dropped her hands to her sides and let out the breath that she had been holding. "I would love some popcorn."

Zoë flinched. Looking down, a smile swept across her face. Hobbling with his crippled paw tucked tightly against his chest, Bart wrapped his body around her leg. He was purring.

Traitor.

Immediately, she scooped the one-eyed cat into her arms. Bart nuzzled against her neck.

Zoë was totally unaffected by the cat's empty eye socket. She cradled him carefully in her arms while tickling his tubby tummy. There was no question; Bart seemed more than happy to enter in to a relationship. Her eyes twinkling, Zoë asked, "And who would this be?"

"That would be my roommate, Bart," Punch said.

Zoë's smile was contagious.

"Have a seat. I'll go put on a shirt—"

Setting Bart onto the couch, she grabbed his arm. "That won't be necessary…"

Kissing her with the primal possession that he'd been holding back, Punch swallowed her into his chest.

Damn, it felt good.

It had been a long day.

Lugowski pulled into the McDonald's fast food restaurant parking lot, turned off the engine, and then loosened his tie. In true cop fashion, he glanced around the lot when strolling toward the restaurant.

Kate West's Mustang was parked two slots down. Mmmm, at least the view would make his Big Mac more appetizing, even though she was probably here with her boyfriend, Holden Reese. No matter, he could still look at her. Hey, surveillance was his forte.

Lugowski shouldered through the door of the restaurant. Mechanically, he took note of the patrons: a business man sat in a booth along the wall to the right of the door checking his text messages while shoving a handful of fries into his mouth before washing it down with a long gulp of his soda. A McDonald's employee swept fries, wrappers, and other debris into a dust pan while wearing a vacant, "I really need a better job" expression on his face. An elderly man read the newspaper along the far wall with a cup of coffee on the table in front of him.

In the corner sat… he narrowed his eyes and cocked his head. Yes, it was Kate West. Her back was to him and her face was buried in her hands. She looked upset—as if she had been crying.

Putting off dinner until later, he ordered two coffees and he made his way toward her. When he approached, he could see a rueful expression on her face. Her beautiful blue eyes were troubled. Her cell phone rested on the table next to an empty coffee cup.

"Need a friend?" he asked.

She looked up. Embarrassed by her watery eyes, she wiped them away with the back of her hands to display a forced smile.

Whoa, this was serious. Sliding into the seat across from her, he placed the coffee on the table in front of her. "Cream, one sweetener, be careful, it's hot," he said.

With trembling lips, she took a cautious sip of the coffee. "Thanks, you remembered," she murmured.

"Of course. You're one of my favorite coffee companions." He tried to lighten her mood.

Afraid to look at him, she stared at the cup. She didn't trust what would come out of her mouth.

Lugowski laced his fingers together and studied her. After a moment, he asked, "How 'bout that dance last night?"

She still did not lift her gaze but let go of a quiet snort.

Trying to coax anything out of her, he continued, "The band wasn't half bad, and the food was pretty good, too. I had to duck out early with all the ruckus. Although, I don't remember seeing you at all. Where were you and Holden hiding out?"

She could feel the flush on her cheeks. She felt like her head would explode with his small talk. Dropping her chin into her hand, she asked, "Where's Ava tonight?"

"At home, I imagine."

"You imagine? You're not sure?"

"I just came off shift. I thought I'd get a bite to eat before I checked in with her." His eyes narrowing, he studied her. He was baffled by her probe. It was plain to see that she was hurting, and he couldn't help but wonder why she wanted to know where Ava was.

Kate bit down hard on her lip. *"Do you want to be responsible for Carl's unhappiness?"* Jen's words of wisdom were coming back to bite. If she didn't get away from Carl quickly, she would soon be spilling her guts. Oh, how she wanted to tell him. How she wanted to rip Ava's world apart like she had done to hers. Instead she muttered, "I'd check in right away, if I were you."

She slid from the booth to make a bee-line for the door.

Stymied, he watched her rush to her car and pull from the lot. Something's up. Damn, he wanted to take her in his arms and kiss away the hurt. Not in this lifetime—probably not in any.

He gathered his coffee and pushed up from the seat when a strong hand clapped onto his shoulder and pressed him back down. Suddenly, he found himself looking at Jack Haliday across the table.

Jack was an ex-Navy SEAL and a colleague. Spending a lot of his time undercover, he worked the gang unit. Wearing a steely look, he picked up Lugowski's coffee from the table and took a big gulp. "Eck, no sugar." He shoved the cup back at Lugowski. He spoke quietly, "I'm giving you a heads-up because I know you've got a thing for Miss West."

An irritated flush started at the base of Lugowski's throat to burn through his cheeks. "What the hell are you talking about?"

"We're watching her boyfriend and that means we're watching her." Jack leaned across the table. "I'm doing you a favor. Don't get too involved. Keep your nose clean, Lugowski."

Lugowski narrowed his eyes. *What the hell?*

Folding his arms over his chest, Jack relaxed against the seat. "What's your girlfriend's name? Ava? She's been working for Reese so she's on the list, too."

Lugowski's spine stiffened. His nostrils flared.

Jack shrugged. "You'd better distance yourself from those two women. If not for your job, for your own safety, 'cause the redhead will kill ya if she finds out about your coffee dates with Kate—not that I blame you, dude, I'm just sayin'."

THE END

... For The Time Being

A note from Cindy McDonald...

*Thank you for reading **Against the Ropes**. I hope you enjoyed the story. I would like to invite you to read an excerpt from the next Unbridled adventure that I have planned for you entitled, **Shady Deals**.*

*As an added bonus, I have also included an excerpt from the first book of my new series, First Force. My new romantic suspense series is expected to debut in the Fall of 2013. The first book from the First Force Series will be titled, **Into the Crossfire**.*

Again, thank you for reading my books, and I hope you enjoy the following two excerpts...

From The Unbridled Series:

Shady Deals

"Take your clothes off," Dr. Holden Reese hissed while closing the door to his veterinarian office at Keystone Downs Thoroughbred Racetrack. He dropped the deadbolt with a clunk into the locked position. His hot gaze slid wantonly over Kate West's slender curves.

A shiver slithered down Kate's spin when she turned to him. She wore a red tank top and a pair of tight Levi Jeans. Her long blonde tresses were pulled back into a casual ponytail. Her silver hoop earrings glinted in the florescent lighting.

While her full lips parted, her eyebrows rose. "Ever heard of sexual harassment, Dr. Reese?" Kate quickly put in.

Unbuckling his belt, he strode toward her. He took the vet box from her hand to set it on a nearby shelving unit, and then pushed her against the block wall. Holden was six-foot-two of solid muscled male. His deep brown eyes burned into her baby blues. Caging her between his arms, he reached back to pull the band that held her hair to let it spill like a golden waterfall about her shoulders. He then fisted his fingers through the locks and tilted her head back to hold her in place. "Oh, I have heard of it, Miss West, and I have every intention of taking you on my desk." He nipped at her earlobe before making his way slowly down her neck. "Do you want to scream?"

Kate's fingers splayed wide on the wall that she was pinned against. Everything female in her clenched at his teasing nips and licks, and the way he smoothed his lips over her hot skin. She could feel her nipples pushing to peaks against the inside of her bra. Letting go of a groan from deep in her throat, she swallowed hard. She rasped, "Do you want me to scream, Dr. Reese?"

Holden smiled against her shoulder. He whispered, "When I make you come." Pressing his lips to hers, he pushed his tongue into her mouth to savor the taste of her while tangling his fingers tighter through her hair. He possessed her.

Pushing up on her toes to capture more from the kiss, Kate wrapped her arms around his waist.

Suddenly, Holden let go of her hair and grabbed her by the shoulders.

Astonished that the kiss had ended so abruptly, Kate blinked back.

"You were stripping..." He stepped back to take in the show about to start.

Recovering quickly, Kate planted her hands on her hips and bit her lip.

Never allowing his gaze to waver, he unbuttoned his jeans, while urging, "The desk is waiting, pretty woman."

"And if I refuse? Will you fire me?"

He lowered his zipper with slow unerring precision. "You won't refuse." Sporting a sinful come-on look, he whipped his T-shirt over his head and tossed it to the floor to bare his sculpted biceps and abs.

"That's not fair!" Kate blurted.

His mouth curved into a wicked smile. "I'll use whatever weapons at my disposal to get you naked. I've been fantasizing since yesterday about doing it on my desk with my sexy little assistant."

Glancing at the desk, Kate noted that it had been cleared for the event.

Holden added, "You won't mention this to your boyfriend, will you?"

Snorting, Kate rolled her eyes at his suggested quirky role-play. What fun. She went along. "He's the jealous type, you know. Not to mention that he could probably beat the snot out of you."

"I'll take my chances." He rolled his right index finger in the air at her. "Let the stripping commence."

Knowing that he rather enjoyed a demure display, she peeked at him through her lashes. Kate slowly slipped her tank over her head and tossed it to the floor—leaving him to ogle her dainty blue lace bra. She unbuttoned her jeans, lowered the zipper bit by bit, and then she shimmied her hips until they slipped down her legs to pool at her feet. Swiftly she kicked them aside.

She could see the column of his erection bulging from his boxer brief through the open fly of his jeans, as she stood before him in a tiny lacey thong and matching bra. He licked his lips. She was driving him crazy. She liked it. Her lips curled at his delicious anticipation.

Slowly, she reached back to unhook the bra, but quickly cupped her breasts in her palms to hold the bra in place. Holden sucked in a deep breath while he watched her bite her lower lip while kneading her breasts in a circular motion before allowing the bra to fall at her feet.

Holden grabbed her hands to restrain them behind her back before she could hook her thumbs through the bands of the thong. Sealing his mouth over hers, he kissed her hard while pulling her against his arousal. "Leave them on," he snarled. He released her hands to grab her buttocks and lift her until she wrapped her legs around his waist. Lips locked, he carried her to the desk where he set her down gently. He murmured, "I don't want to hurry my fantasy. I want to savor it, baby."

Kate pulled away from the kiss. She whispered, "I don't know. My boyfriend will be coming to pick my up soon for the bonfire party at our farm tonight. He doesn't like it when I'm late."

Holden's eyes brightened. "I almost forgot about that." He brushed a lock of hair from her cheek with the pad of his thumb. His eyes narrowed when he asked, "Is the whole party taking place outside?"

Confused by the question, Kate cocked her head. "Yes."

"No one will be in the barn?"

"No."

Carefully, he laid her across the desk. He admired her dusty pink nipples standing at attention while waiting for him to nip. The sinful grin returned to his handsome face. "Mmmm, another fantasy just came to mine, Miss West: The rugged cowboy breezes into town and seduces the sassy cowgirl in the hayloft."

Shaking her head, Kate chuckled. "Please, one fantasy at a time or I won't be able to keep up, cowboy." She was right.

He decided to fulfill this fantasy right now. There would be plenty of time this evening for the other—if he could get her alone in the loft. He smiled to himself thinking of a clever way to lure her into the loft of her father's Thoroughbred farm, Westwood.

Dropping both of his hands on either side of her, he lowered his face to kiss her between her breasts when the cell phone in his hip pocket began to ring and vibrate. He groaned.

Kate giggled. "That's a mood killer," she muttered.

"Not for me." He ran his tongue over her stiff nipple.

"Aren't you going to answer it?"

He stilled. "No."

"Holden, someone could be in trouble. You should at least look at the number."

"Really?"

"Really."

Again his extremely capable and compassionate vet assistant was right. He let out a frustrated sigh as he yanked the phone from his pocket to look at the screen: Chip Walker.

Reaching across her body, he grabbed the handle to the middle drawer of the desk, pulled it open, flipped the phone in, and then slammed the drawer shut. "It's no one important enough to interrupt this moment." He looked into her crystal blue eyes full of desire. Raking his fingers through her hair, he said, "Nothing is more important than you are." His fingers slipped from her hair, down her neck until he cupped her breast in his hand. "Now where was I?"

ᔄ   ᔭ   ᔄ   ᔭ

Chip Walker thumbed the *END* button on his cell phone with a frustrated sigh. Doc Reese hadn't answered his calls or his texts in three days. Reese was getting too independent. He wasn't respecting his authority. Reese could blow his whole operation to smithereens. The operation had been compromised only a month ago, but he had managed to dodge that bullet. He couldn't afford another mishap. Reese needed to conform. Reese needed to fall in line.

***PLEASE NOTE: Changes could be made to the excerpt that you just read during the editing process of publishing **Shady Deals**.*

From Cindy's new series
First Force

Into the Crossfire

The phones rang incessantly while detectives sat at their desks drinking way too much coffee. Their suit jackets were slung over the backs of their chairs and the surface of their desks were scattered with paperwork that had spilled over from the bins that sat on the corner. The large dank room that housed the gang unit of the Rosemount Police Department was a tornado of hustle.

Eyeing the red blinking button coming from the phone on his desk, Jack Haliday crooned into his cell phone, "I love you too, baby girl," as he listened to her response, the corners of his mouth kicked up, "yeah, daddy will be home for birthday cake soon."

"Haliday…" Captain Lutz called from the doorway of his office. Jack glanced over his shoulder, "In my office, A-SAP." The captain said with a hitch of his chin toward his door.

Uh, oh.

"Can you put mommy on the phone?" Jack urged his little daughter, and after listening to her tiny voice call out to her mother, and after the sound of juggling the phone from the toddler's hand, Laura was on the line.

"You'll be home by seven?" Laura asked. It wasn't really a question, it was an order.

"I should be. Gotta go, Lutz just called me into his office."

"Ahhh, Jack…" she moaned.

He could feel the roll of her eyes on the other end of the line. He understood her frustration. Jack was a member of the gang squad, which translated into long hours and sometimes weeks away from home on assignment. He was hoping that's not what the captain wanted from him today. Today was Lillian's fourth birthday, and he didn't want to miss a moment. He'd already missed so much. "I know, sweetheart, hopefully it's just a question about some paperwork that I've turned in. You know, some T that wasn't crossed or I that wasn't dotted. Don't worry, I'll be there." He promised while listening to another sigh. Laura was having her doubts and he didn't blame her.

"Haliday…" Lutz called from his desk.

"Gotta go, love you." Jack said, as he disconnected the call, shoving the phone into his pocket. On his way to the captain's office he danced around a fellow detective who was attempting to balance a full mug of coffee.

Pursing his lips, Captain Patrick Lutz looked up at the six-foot-two muscular man filling the doorway. Jack leaned a broad shoulder against the jamb scrubbing his fingers over his bristly face. He hadn't had time to shave this morning and his beard was already filling his jaw line. Although it was short, his dark hair was a thick nest of waves. His blue stripped tie dangled loose from his unbuttoned collar and his sleeves were rolled to his elbows. Captain Lutz gestured for Jack to have a seat.

Lutz looked the way he always looked: tired. His white shirt was slightly wrinkled. He had loosened his tie and unbuttoned his collar as well. His desk was a hotchpotch of paperwork and folders. The desk was situated in front of a window that overlooked the main street of Rosemount. The window was draped in dust and grime. It looked as though the window washers hadn't made a visit in weeks, maybe more. Cut backs. The sound of honking horns and bus engines from the street below filtered through the dirty window—the ebb and flow of the city street.

Jack eased into an old leather chair across from the captain's desk praying that he wouldn't have to make that phone call to Laura explaining that he would be missing Lillian's party because Lutz had an it can't wait assignment. Jack watched Lutz fidget in his seat for a few moments, tapping his fingers on the desk, and then he looked Jack square in the eye. The crease in his forehead deepened. His gaze was filled with concern. Picking up a paperclip, he leaned forward resting his elbows on the desk, while flipping the paperclip between his fingers. Something was up. Shit, no birthday party for him this evening. Lutz began, "I've got some bad news, Jack. Gunner has been spotted in the area, two blocks from your house."

Jack's spine stiffened. His jaw clenched. A bad feeling skittered up the nape of his neck.

Three years ago...

Jack's undercover operation had just gone totally FUBAR. He had been working the mission for months missing most of his Laura's pregnancy. He had successfully infiltrated a notorious biker gang, the Nomads. Slow and meticulously he managed to gain the gang leader, Gunner's trust. So close, he was so close to extracting all the evidence that he needed to blow the gang wide open, when it all went to hell...

Gunner and his gang had been known to rendezvous at an abandoned mansion, located in a ravaged strip-mined dead land in the middle of every-lovin' nowhere, where they traded illegal weapons, dealt drugs, and dabbled in a little human trafficking, for good measure.

When the Nomads arrived at the mansion they came upon an abandoned pickup truck parked in the driveway, and a rusted-out aged Impala around back. The discovery sent Gunner into a tantrum. Immediately the grounds were spinning within a hornet's nest of raging bikers shooting their Uzi's into the air racing through the property in search of the intruders.

After hours of searching and coming up empty, Jack was relieved that whoever had violated Gunner's mansion was nowhere to be found.

Jack had just taken quiet refuge in the darkness of the stairwell in the east turret wishing this op was over. As an ex Navy SEAL, he usually kept his hair cut close and his face shaved clean. Except now his dark hair brushed his broad shoulders, and the freakin' beard itched like hell. The quiet he had sought out was suddenly interrupted by the sound of a thud from the corridor overhead. Cautiously he made his way up the rickety stairs that creaked and gave beneath his boots...

The loud squeal from the rollers beneath Lutz's chair as he pushed from his desk brought Jack out of his funk. The captain shuffled around the desk to sit on the corner with his leg draped over the side. Crossing his arms over his chest, he continued, "The sonofabitch has been underground for three years. I've had a feeling that he was biding his time, trying to make us comfortable with his absence. I'm going to put an extra patrol on your street to keep a closer eye on Laura and Lil."

"To hell with that, Lutz. I'm getting them the hell out of there as soon as I can."

Running a hand over his balding head and then back down over his weary eyes, Lutz said, "Yeah, well that's just it, Jack, you've got an assignment starting tomorrow—"

Jack jerked to his feet, "Ah, c'mon Lutz! You just told me that the murdering sonofabitch that got away three years ago is hanging around my house, and you're sending me out on assignment? My girls will be sitting ducks!"

"I just told you, I'm going to put extra patrols to watch over them. Do you think I want anything to happen to Laura and Lil?"

"Extra patrols? You think that's gonna stop Gunner? Shit, he'll eat them for breakfast and then have my girls for lunch! No! I'm staying to watch over my family."

"I understand that it's a bad situation at best, but you've got to trust us on this, Jack. We'll keep Laura and Lil safe. Not to mention we've got a team watching for Gunner to move. He goes anywhere near your house or your family and we'll take him out."

"You've got a team on Gunner? How long has this been going on? Why wasn't I called to that team? I want to be in on this, captain!" Jack bit out.

"That's exactly what Gunner expects. He's looking for you to be on the investigation. No, you'll take this other assignment and let the team do their job while you're doing yours."

"What team? Who's on the team and what have they got so far?"

"It's Fairchild's team, and they haven't got much. Gunner's a cool customer. He's lying low. They've only spotted him once, but if he makes a move, we'll be there." The captain let out a frustrated breath as he glanced at the clock above the door. "It's six-thirty, Jack. You'd best get home for Lil's birthday. I'll brief you on your assignment tomorrow."

Jack didn't move. Fairchild had a damned good team, nonetheless his gut churned over the danger his family was in, and the memory of the assignment that starting the wheels in motion **three years ago...**

Jack peered from the shadows of the turret into the dark corridor to find, Buck, one of his "fellow bikers" with his gun trained on a man standing protectively in front of a woman. "What's going on, Buck?" he asked from the dark doorway.

"I was sleeping against that wall there. This guy tripped over my feet." Buck said over his shoulder. Jack stepped in to have a closer look. That's when he recognized the man, Lieutenant Carl Lugowski. Lugowski worked the homicide department, while Jack worked the gang squad for the Rosemount Police Department. It was time for some serious damage control.

Roughly Jack grabbed the woman pulling her into the light. He could see her trying to swallow her fear. Lugowski's jaw clenched so tightly that the skin rippled over the bone.

Jack had only met Lugowski a handful of times, moreover at those times he was clean shaven and clean cut. Jack was well aware that his fellow officer did not recognize him. "Whoa, she's a nice piece of tail. I'll take her to Gunner," Jack said, drawing his gun. Protectively, Lugowski stepped forward. Jack greeted him with his gun, "Don't worry, dude, we won't leave you out. You can watch."

"Wait a goddamned minute!" Buck protested, "I found her and I'm gonna take her. Gunner might let me have her when he's done."

"And he might sell her to his customers that come for the guns tomorrow. Look at her, she's prime, man." Jack said, as she jerked trying to break his hold. Jack snorted, "Feisty too, she'll bring a damned good price."

Jack stabbed Lugowski in the shoulder with his gun, "Walk, asshole," he harshly instructed, wishing he could covertly inform him of his identity, except Buck was following right along. Jack would have to dispose of the old grubby biker. Collateral damage.

As Lugowski strode off the last step, he swung his fist upward smacking Jack in the nose. Blood spewed from his nostrils, as he flung backward into Buck, while releasing the blonde's arm, careful not to pull the trigger of his gun. The plan was futile. Buck's semi-automatic engaged. Bullets ripped through the tower ricocheting madly off the round walls. Lugowski grabbed the blonde's arm making a mad dash down the corridor that spilled into the side yard, while Buck sprayed the interior of the turret with gunfire and cursing.

Jack swiped his hand at Buck trying to grab his gun, only the old biker possessed more agility than Jack had given him credit for. Buck slammed the butt of the gun across Jack's temple knocking him backward down the three or four steps. Jack landed on his back hard, dazed, cracking his head against the cement floor. Buck jumped over him calling out warning to his sleeping comrades that there had been a breach in security.

Everything went black...

"Jack..." Captain Lutz's terse call shook him from his memory. He looked up to find Lutz staring at him with a raised brow. Lutz insisted, "Go home, Jack. You'll actually be on time for once, now go."

Like a lightning bolt out of the blue, an overwhelming urgency to be with Laura and Lil coiled through him. He scrambled out of Lutz's office to his desk, grabbed his jacket, and pulled his cell phone from the pocket, thumbing the numbers as he raced toward the door. The phone on the other end began to ring as he slipped between two police officers at the top of the stairs to make his way down. The phone rang, and rang, and rang. Driblets of sweat formed on his brow. She wasn't answering. Laura wasn't answering the phone. WTF? She should be there. She should be setting the cake on the table, pressing the candles through the sugary icing, while trying to keep Lil at a distance. He glanced down at his watch: six-forty.

Jumping, he skipped the last two steps, nodding apologetically to a female detective that he almost plowed into. As he pressed through the doors of the precinct, he thumbed the REDIAL button. The phone rang and rang. "C'mon Laura, answer!" He ground out, as he jogged through the parking lot approaching his SUV. There was a juggling sound, a clunk, and then a tiny giggle followed by, "Hewo..."

Jack slammed his feet against the pavement to a halt. He dropped his head against the door of his vehicle, pressing his eyes closed, thank God. "Lillian?"

"Daddy! Birfday cake! Birfday cake! Mommy's got candles!" The toddler couldn't contain her delight.

Jack let go of the breath that he'd been holding. His shoulders slumped in relief. He smiled, "Tell mommy that I'm on my way home."

"Bye, bye, daddy!" she squealed. Before he heard the thump of the phone onto the receiver he heard her call out, "Daddy's coming!"

He pressed the END button, and then slid into the SUV. They were okay. For now.

Please note: Changes may be made to the excerpt that you have just read during the editing stage of publishing **Into the Crossfire.

About the Author

Cindy McDonald

For twenty-six years my life whirled around a song and a dance: I was a professional dancer/choreographer for most of my adult life and never gave much thought to a writing career until 2005. Don't ask me what happened, but suddenly I felt drawn to my computer to write about things I have experienced (greatly exaggerated upon of course) with my husband's Thoroughbreds and the happenings at the racetrack.

Surprised? Why didn't I write about my experiences with dance? Eh, believe it or not life at the racetrack is more...racy. The drama is outrageous—not that dancers don't know how to create drama, believe me, they do; but race trackers just seem to get more down and dirty with it which makes great story telling—great fiction.

I didn't start out writing books, The Unbridled Series started out as a TV drama, and the Hollywood readers loved the show. The problem was we just couldn't sell it. So one of the readers said to me, "Cindy, don't be stupid. Turn your scripts into a book series." and so I did!

In May of 2011 I took the big leap and exchanged my dancin' shoes for a lap top—I retired from dance. It was a scary proposition, I was terrified, but I had the full support of my husband, Saint Bill. It has been a huge change for me. I went from dancing hard five hours a night to sitting in front of a computer. I still work-out and I take my dog, Harvey, for a daily run. I have to or I'd be as big as a house. Do I miss dance? Sometimes I do. I miss my students. I miss choreographing musicals, but I love my books and I love sharing them with you.

To read excerpts from future books, view book trailers, and keep up with everything that is Unbridled, please visit Cindy's website at: www.cindymcwriter.com

CHECK OUT ALL THE BOOKS IN THE UNBRIDLED SERIES

Make a note: never agitate a madman. Successful Thoroughbred trainer Mike West just made that mistake, and he's gonna pay—more than he ever realized. But it's all in the family; his sister, Kate, has been the object of the madman's desire on the social network site "My Town". Her constant rejections have infuriated him. People who seem to be in his way start turning up dead, and he's got Kate and Mike next on his list! In the first book of The Unbridled Series Cindy McDonald introduces you to the world of Thoroughbred racing, while taking her cast of characters for a wild ride through a maniac's mind.

SPELLBOUND!

Wow!! I could not put this book down. This is the first book in the Unbridled series. From the first chapter I knew this series is a keeper. I am spellbound by Cindy McDonald's story telling and the twist and blind curves this story takes you on. This book really makes you ques tion who you are chatting with online and question our justice system. It's wise to remember things are not always what they appear.

Reviewer: Wanted:Readers blog

A Touch of Evil!

George is an absolutely horrible person. I hated him from the get go and, as I read, hungrily awaited his demise—he is the epitome of evil. I don't care if he is a little bit psycho or if his mother made him this way—EVIL. It amazes me that McDonald was able to evoke such strong, passionate feelings of abhorrence from me over a fictional character, but it is a testament of McDonald's writing ability! I liked the pacing of the story, especially as the action picks up almost as soon as the story begins. It was very well done.

Reviewer: A Book Vacation blog

YOU DON'T WANT TO MISS HOT COCO!!!

Coco Beardmore is sizzling and she's landed in Mike West's lap. Trouble is Coco's middle name is chaos! Her driving skills are a real bang—into Mike's horse trailer. Her seduction will set the room on fire—the kitchen that is.

What's worse is her Thoroughbred's ability to mimic their owner's habit of screwing things up. It's enough to drive a normally calm and collected Mike West to the very edge.

But Mike's not the only one having trouble with women. His father, Eric has bitten off more than he can chew and he's about to get spit out by two women: one that he's in love with and one that thinks he's in love with her.

FUNNY & HEARTWARMING

Hot Coco is not just a steamy romance novel - but is funny, and heart warming, and really touches the heart. I love that this story takes place on a Thoroughbred farm. I love horses! I love Cindy McDonald's writing style which is fast, easy, and keeps you turning the pages to find out what happens next. The characters are believable and totally relatable. This book is the second book in the series. I haven't read the first book, but Hot Coco was good as a standalone. I plan to download the first book in the series - and anything else Cindy McDonald puts out.

Reviewer: Jennifer Golub
Waiting for Sunday to Drown

UNEXPECTEDLY INSIGHTFUL

The book is fun, quirky, unexpectedly insightful, funny, and warm. A truly good read.

Reviewer: Mindy Wall
Books, Books, and More Books

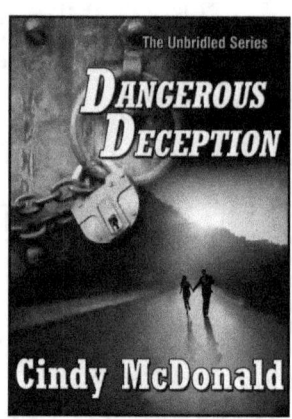

Vic Deveaux's glory days as a winning jockey have ended, but he refuses to accept that pile of horse hockey! When the West family asks Vic to take an easier position at their Thoroughbred farm, Westwood, he becomes enraged and teams up with two greedy stable hands in a scheme to kidnap the youngest son, Shane.

Things turn ugly when Vic discovers that his new-found friends have murder on their minds. Suddenly Vic finds himself between a rock and a hard place. He has betrayed his good friend, Eric West, but will he participate in his son's murder as well?

Not content to sit at home and wait for her men to bring her brother home, Kate West convinces homicide detective, Carl Lugowski, to check out a hunch at an old abandoned mansion. Soon they're trapped in a hornet's nest of a notorious biker gang.

Oh yeah, Vic's deception has placed the West family in more danger than they know what to do with!

PLOT CHARGED WITH SUSPENSE AND DANGER

Only author Cindy McDonald can deliver a plot so charged and filled with suspense, danger, and surprises to the West family. **Dangerous Deception** *will keep you glued in your saddle until you cross the finish line or read the last page!*

Reviewer: Fran Lewis

Fantastic Thriller!

This full book took off like a truck on an open road and the reader was just holding on for dear life, and I loved it! The mix of bikers, drugs, horses and money made for a fantastic thriller where you hoped that good would win, but the reader wasn't quite sure with every bend in the road. I fell in love with this family of horse breeders and think that this series could be a success with the family at the center.

Reviewer: Kritters Ramblings

Catch up with Cindy McDonald & Everything Unbridled at
www.cindymcwriter.com

Hey! You can view book trailers at the site as well.

Cindy would love to hear from you!
unbridledseries@gmail.com